In The Side Pocket

In The Side Pocket

D.B. Smith

This Volume is Dedicated to Trillis Hitchcock

The Mother of Gayle Smith

This I remember of Trillis, now deceased:

TRILLIS KISSED ME

One thing I remember,
Under the roof of my home.
Entering on a visit,
Mama did not just say hello.
Something a little more exquisite
Entered with her on a visit—
A kiss along with, "Hi"
Meant she really missed me.
And, I knew she really loved me
When Trillis kissed me.

Contents

THE CARRADINE BRAND 137

D. B. Smith

✖✖✖

FIFTY LITTLE JOYS AND SORROWS

THE GREY BUICK AND OTHER STORIES

THE GREY BUICK

A forlornly looking grey Buick stood on a far corner of a back lot. Its tires were low. It was dented, scratched, scrapheap oriented, crusted with rust from neglect and compromised in every way possible. It was a candidate to be burned at a movie location under a new coat of paint. A broken grill looked weirdly gruesome and grinned wickedly beneath two headlamp eyes.

The engine started and sort of purred, then sputtered from a sticking choke, then quit. Three minutes later, it started again.

"We can fix her," said Charley Anniston to his college bound son, Peter. "We" meant the two of them together, side by side, inside, of an April, rain or shine.

NECKLESS

Off white pearls were strung upon silver string upon a mannequin, neck and bodice. Exquisitely were they hung in odd- length doubles. Displayed they were in a pawn shop window. The pawnbroker waived his profit and marked them down to 159.00.

One year ago the pearls had been carried away from a mansion within a robber's black carry-all bag. Not worth a ransom, it would seem. Alive, they would have died from boredom.

A woman wearing rundown heels on second hand flats, peered through glass at them. Her head rested very near bent shoulders. Her reflection twinned her black coat and flower print dress and resisted what her heart became set upon, looking like the queen.

A trade was made. Her useless wedding ring from another year took the place of the string of pearls. She stood in silent admiration in front of a window pane. She felt the deft unclasping and watched in silent sadness as the pearls dropped into the bag of a running thief.

They were gone she knew, not to be recovered.

Shock set in, then relief. The moment was worth the ring. Softly, she began to sing.

SCATTER

The leaves talked about their ride upon the wind to a resting, nesting place. They wore red hats upon their brown, grey-brown, yellow scalloped faces. Their chatter was a rustle upon a breath of breeze.

"Up there, I came from the third one from the left."

"Mine is number four. See, my brother hangs on tightly. He won't let go before a stronger wind blows him out of sight. He'll look like a yellow kite!"

More scattered toss of mix greeted them and snuggled close for warmth to wait for broom and rake. They dryly wept for each other's sake.

These refugees from trees were doomed. Bonfires made ashes for the garden when these leaves hit the ground. Some from Ashes that in spring would rebound. New leaves would green and brown and fall and scatter and settle and speak a language old as Earth and take turns telling of birth and rebirth.

A child of another century landed playfully among the progeny. Another child and another were gleeful for an hour in a pile resplendent, gathered, and showered with new scatter.

GRAIL TEST

A place to work gave this man his satisfaction. If that work afforded him physical activity, shirt off in the sun, he could go all day to pleasurable tiredness and love doing it. His name was Howard. No coward, he had seen his share of battle in the Great War. He moved from Gandy dancer to freight handler to farm hand to dam builder to grounds keeper to munitions handler in all of forty years. Then night time janitor took him to retirement.

In a quiet patient thirty years he took his Holy Grail to his year 95. His walks were long, and rewarded him with rocks that attracted him. Some conversations with shop keepers were long. Stroke rehab meant slower walks and wavering strokes to paint and write with a right hand unused to a lefty's tasks. Exercise was life giving. Balance was important and practiced. A diligent churchgoer, he kept things of the spirit in good health. Only to himself did he write once of doubt.

To the end, he kept his own council, stuck to a well honed ethical code in thought and conduct. In all that time, he only raised his voice with "Jeepers!" or " cheese and crackers!" or "Darn!".

He did see 96 with illness and lessening of his own indomitable spirit. He defied death, perhaps with one of his own choosing. Did he hold his breath? Only he would ever know.

THE BLONDE GENTLEMAN'S PREFERENCE

He was tall. His hair was naturally blonde. Jake Goodman's Roman nose resembled one reassembled by the gods to give him charm and disarming engagement upon entering a room. The stares were from female eyes; and he could have his pick for entertaining conversation. He stood with a glass held loosely between the middle fingers of his right hand.

Jake, though nonchalant, was not a rake. He did, however, want a companion for the evening. He surveyed the room for someone who seemed unattached, someone whose repartee would walk over to him and give him a high five feeling. He would settle for something less if he had to.

She turned, laughing, away from a group of three women and gave him a mirrored image of the picture of the birthday girl.

He was there because....well, her brother had invited him. Thom was busy in an upstairs room and had left him to carry on alone. A thirty-five year old confirmed bachelor locked onto the eyes of a seventeen year old with black bobbed hair, an open mouthed smile that showed gleaming white teeth. Her complexion was pink with a hint of a scar above the right brow.

He did not have to move. She paused, came closer, and asked if he were having a good time.

"Of course. And, how is the birthday girl enjoying the evening?"

"Swell. It's swell."

A light touch of scent surrounded her. Elegantly gowned in white taffeta with lavender trim, she drew looks and envy that was palpable. Then she moved on, pulling herself into talky-talk in various groups and twos.

Ah! the gentleman in the grey suit!

"Hi, I'm Jake. You're a snappy dresser."

"I'm Timothy Brown. I'm just jake as well. Can I get you another drink?"

"I'll go with you."

They took refreshment from a tray. Jake pointed to the stairs. Timothy took his arm and they sidled up the steps. No one thought it strange. Everyone knew the blonde preferred a gentleman.

THE OLD COWBOY'S EVERYTHING SHOP

Fifteen years ago a footloose, forty-five year old cowpoke rode into the mountain town of Duggan in the back of a pickup truck. The end of the road was punctuated with a parking space and a "This is it." from the driver, Willard Grimes.

Stuart Chance dropped his duffle and climbed out. Nothing was familiar. He was disoriented in direction until the summer sun filled his eyes with brightness. The roadway was north and south. The row of shops faced east. Shadows had begun to form.

Stuart's pocket watch read 4:10. Lordie! His back and shoulders ached. His butt was sore. The effects of the wind at fifty-five miles an hour and the three hour ride tore at him; and he carried the look of pain in his eyes. Now, he was at the mercy of strangers. That meant for the first time in his adult life he would have to ask for help.

Fifteen years he sat in the town's barber shop, sweeping, cleaning, and regaling customers with the stories that made up his early roundup days. He was good for business. He had a free cot in the back behind a curtain. He lived frugally and saved his earnings at compound interest. The last five years he apprenticed. When the boss barber, Pop Finley, passed away, Stuart bought the shop. Now he was a successful businessman who told stories without end. As a customer got up from the chair, he would ask, "Is that everything?"

UNLIKELY CHAMPIONSHIP

The girls of Middle Bluff High managed in a way just short of miraculous to field a basketball team. One girl was a chubby eighth grader. Her first dribble was high with a palmed ball that would have to be tamed. Susan Mesh filled her uniform, front, back and every other way. Peaches Gardener was too thin to be seen in profile. Miss "no muscle" got the ball only half way to the basket. She was short in shorts that barely stayed up. In ninth grade math she sat behind Louise Seffler, nicknamed "Giant". The teacher had to call her name to be sure she was present. Louise would plug the middle. Her hook shot was often an air ball. She stayed late fixing it.

Chick Bailey played garage door hoops with the boys. She would be a player coach and play maker. She would have to help shape up the others.

"Glad" Phillips went out for the exercise. She was a clown and would be hard to discipline. She would, at best, be the bench player in the estimation of the assistant basketball coach, Dante Williams.

Betty Stang, a senior, would fill in as the fifth player and fill her jersey and fill the floor with her defense.

Dante impressed upon them that fouling out would mean they would be playing short if it happened twice.

Yes, they won against four other rag-tag teams and would play for the championship against the skills of the girls of Camp Payne, who were all college recruits. The pep talk emphasized, "Get all the points you can. Don't worry about the score. You've come a long way. Just go for it! Bring it on! Let's go!"

They were good at the free throw line. Yes, they lost, but, only by four points. A standing ovation was given both teams.

Wait 'til next year. "Glad" Phillips had gone from clown to a student of the game, absorbing everything from the sidelines. Stang would graduate. Glad would be a starter. And, best of all, Dante would have no shortage of girls from which to choose. He would probably have a B squad.

Stang was recruited by Connecticut.

TROUBLE

This is not the story of River City. A kayaker on the Colorado River is in the story, and, if he were not in trouble, there would be no story.

Jesus Sanchez lost sight of the river during a portage caused by a falls of some depth with turbulent water beneath. His right-turn at a bend led to lost, to berating himself for "going it alone" confidence. He was skilled; but a lapse of concentration had him disoriented in a way he swore would never happen to him. He had read of lost hikers and wondered at their vacuity.

His cell phone emergency call was unanswered by anything but dead air. Damn it! He was lost. He needed to gather himself and work out a plan. No fires meant no fires! He could not build one large enough to be spotted from the air. A mirror would come in handy. This was supposed to be three hours of white water then home. His brother would meet him at James crossing. If he could not find the river, any search would miss him.

A man of faith, he prayed and camped where he was. His overturned kayak could shelter him from rain.

The sunset had brilliant hues that held lavender that darkened with the fading light. Then, as he lay awake, his prayer was answered. The river had to be west. In the morning he would walk away from the rising sun. The bend in the west flowing river could mean extra miles of walking. His sealed pouch of power bars would assuage hunger. His logic was faulty. He could never walk west to meet a west flowing river.

He woke early. He took the time to break off saplings and use the bark to make a travois for the kayak.

Noon surely should have brought him to the river.
Why had this ex Boy Scout not been prepared? Where
was the compass? Where was the river? Where was his
brother? He tried his cell phone again and again during
his travail until it went dead.

There was a peak in the distance; but surely it was
south. If he climbed, just maybe he could spot the river.
Hope seemed to be all he had left.

Three days of wilderness had him questioning his
sanity. His confidence had been shattered. He no longer
planned to find a way out. Resignation set in. He had
eaten the last of the power bars. He was dirty and
disheveled. It was useless to gather rock for a ring of
fire. No compass and no matches. Common sense had
deserted him in the beginning; and assessing his loss
would only add to the morose feeling he would carry with
him as he sat to await the end.

Near dark, search dogs found him. His brother
hugged him as they both wept out of joy. This prodigal
was gathered to his father's house—with a barbeque in
celebration.

THE FLIGHT OF IGGY WANNA

A large iguana had flights of fancy. It lay lizard-like and dreamed of flying. It relished the name given it by casual observers, Iggy. In his waking hours he hissed a whispered, "Iggy wanna, Iggy wanna fly." He looked up at gulls and hawks and eagles and cursed his outcast state. Why could he not be feathered and winged and soaring instead of lumber-some and cumbersome, scaled and ugly, flicking a long tongue for survival?

Vivid dreams had him diving toward earth to snatch a prey and take it skyward. Drifting on favorable winds, he circled and wheeled, moving wings occasionally to change course. What he saw himself doing was only for the birds.

One day an eagle landed nearby, a little off course for its craggy perch. Iggy got excited, hissing, "Iggy wanna.....Iggy wanna....Iggy wanna fly!" The wise eagle squeaked, "I will see what I can do." And it flew out of sight.

The next day, the eagle returned with many of its high flight friends. They gathered around Iggy. They began to latch onto him with their talons. When each had a secure hold, they took off. Higher and higher they flew, "Wafting on laughter silvered wings"*, Iggy had his dream come true; and he lived out the rest of his life content to be an iguana.

*Words from "High Flight" by Pilot officer Gillespie Magee, RCAFC

HANDSOME FARM GIRL

Plain and tall best described Sara Williamson. Hers was a life of hogs and sows and dairy cows and cabbages and kings. Hers was a life of digging for a garden and fence mending. Her slim frame had the muscles to prove it. She was thirty-two and content to drive a pickup and tractor-plow a field for sunflowers. That crop paid the taxes.

Her parents were gone, two months apart, in their sleep. She was now as much a part of that land as they had been. Though not a churchgoer, she knelt each night to pray as they had. That long transition disappeared into antiquity but served her in time of need. At this vesper time she could bring back Grandma Smith to whisper words of comfort and solace.

The recipes of her mother's mother came to mind. She had no one to cook for; but she savored the notion that one day she would. Soon, she hoped.

She mulled over a couple of proposals. But, both suitors seemed eager to acquire her land. That would never happen.

It was spring. The lilac bushes took on the scent of a fresh bath. Sara, too, seemed to be in flower. Her prayer turned to someone to wrap herself around and engage in fireworks long before the Fourth of July. He would have to want only her.

That evening Grandma Smith said, "Look beyond the gate. That one won't come to you."

Sara called Betty Gardener and her husband, James, who came out to watch over the spread for two days. She packed a bag and drove to the train station. She boarded the limited to Boston where she hoped an accent waited for her. Her frivolous getaway might as well result in something romantic.

She came home defeated. She could not bring herself to fling herself at some stranger. She spent her time in the walking town sleeping and eating. The highlight of her overnight was a sampling of oysters and lobster and looking at the ocean. She could only believe she had escaped once more.

It was a hot summer day in July that Arden Cooper stopped to ask directions to the Cooper place he had just inherited.

She saw this as her last opportunity; and she took it. She invited him in and invited him over and over and over. She wooed him with subtle gestures of friendship.

He had his place and ran it well. It outshone her little farm. But he always praised her efforts. He finally asked her to marry him. He agreed to a pre-nup that stated her farm was hers in perpetuity. Her children would inherit from her. She would go to work her farm and come to his in the evening. Arden was that caring kind of man who was both unselfish and adoring.

At sixty-five Arden's heart attack killed him. Sara survived quietly in tune with her grandma. She sold Arden's place and went home.

THE OLD FORD DIED

Charley Ford owned one. Nothing was for it but that he would restore a Model T and keep it the rest of his life. He would never regret the twenty thousand mint condition it had cost him. He kept it oiled and running like new. He pampered it beyond what he would for a new baby.

Candace Ford took her husband's toy to heart. They toured to summer antique car shows, the Ford tucked into its own trailer and pulled behind a cab-over. Their hearts raced one night near Minneapolis. Candace woke to the sound of the pickup motor running. Charley slept undisturbed. Her scream woke him. They went to the window in time to see the rig ease into traffic.

Fortunately the trailer was found by a patrolman in a cruiser, blocks from the motel. The seal was intact, the Ford untouched. Only the cab-over was missing.

The trailer was towed back to the motel. The theft was reported to their insurance company. Their outing ruined, they paid for an extra night's lodging.

The APB brought results. Two teens were stopped and arrested. Charley and Candace returned to Sioux City, South Dakota. Ever after they slept in the cab-over at a truck stop-with a shot gun and under the security of a car alarm.

When Charley died, the Model T quit working. It would never run again.

GIVE THEM THEIR DUE

Jimmy Dooley went religiously to the gym to work out. His youth found him in Golden Gloves tournaments with an enviable record for wins and a couple of TKO'S because his opponents failed to answer the bell. Now, he kept his body in the shape he worked so hard to achieve.

So many police academy graduates did only enough to fit into their uniforms and changed sizes with age. Jimmy did all things wise to be prepared for any challenge. He was secure enough to moonlight as a model. There was not an eluding perp. he could not literally run down. He carried the banner and headlined for charity boxing matches.

His toughest conquest, however, was skinny, pintsized, and overmatched in any physical activity. He would never hold his own against the bully who was his nemesis. He was a weakling.

Jimmy's nephew, Ryan, was fearful when threatened and meekly gave in to demands. He was the runt of the litter and someday would wear tailored suits and be somebody. He was smart. He was the classic student who had valedictorian stamped on his forehead from the time he asked for a microscope for Christmas at age seven. He took piano lessons. There wasn't a girl he couldn't beat with his hand in the air to answer a question.

Then, with an epiphany under his belt, Jimmy hijacked Ryan, took him to his empty garage and bolted the door. The garage was not completely empty. There was a weight bench and a set of weights, graduated sets of dumbbells, a box of skip ropes, a chin up bar., an exercise mat: these Jimmy supplied for the purpose of doing a makeover, of transforming Ryan, who would be knocked into a cocked hat if he said no.

Ryan was scared. He shook. This bully was not going to let him off the hook. Tears came and ran down his cheeks. He looked into the cold, resolute eyes of Jimmy and fainted.

Ryan was brought to by a splash of cold water and his regimen began.

After six months of a merciless reluctant pursuit of muscle, Ryan was suddenly confronted by a gloved fist by Jimmy who gave him a pair of boxing gloves. "Put 'em on and go for it!" Jimmy tapped him just hard enough to knock him down. Again and again. He called the kid a momma's boy.

Fists flying and rushing his tormentor, Ryan assaulted the adult. A blow actually landed on Jimmy's face. Ryan was ready for lessons.

A year later, Ryan's name came up as a contender for the Golden Gloves junior championship match. The bullies had witnessed the transformation over time and had quietly faded into the woodwork. All of them knew Ryan now could give them their due.

GOD IS INTO PEACHES

"Peaches for sale!" Nice, ripe peaches for sale!"
God heard the strangled yell of a hawker on the
street, a yell that seemed to come from every street
corner in many tones and variations. God was pleased
that the nectar was of His own choosing.

"Peaches for sale!" The man whose pushcart was
heaped high advertised how juicy they were when his
chin whiskers shone as he sampled his own ware.
Jonathon White sold apples occasionally; but he was best
rewarded for his peaches, homegrown and delivered to
his "vehicle for show" that could move unobtrusively
upon walkways, from place to place. Corners were sure
to draw crowds.

God thought back to the age of creation. That
perfect peach, however, was only a fruit, something God
had pronounced good. It was good to be where peddlers
sold peaches. Time and place were not significant.
Jonathon made God uneasy.

Jonathon White complained the peaches on the
bottom were always bruised and had to be greatly
discounted late in the day. They were good only for
preserves. He was a religious man and railed at God
because he was not requited for his faithfulness. God
simply let him down.

God knew his mind. It was revealed a thousand
fold every moment. This man would have to be taught a
new faith. A clown face and a baggy checkered outfit
presented, themselves to Jonathon, dancing around the
produce cart. The clown reached for one peach after
another and tossed it into the air until all were being
juggled in one giant circle, much to the amazement of
spectators. The peaches returned unblemished to the
cart exactly in reverse order. All formerly bottom
peaches were on top.

At the end of the day Jonathon realized a bigger profit than ever before. His tiredness was assuaged; and he was ready to rejoice, until he thought of old Jane who would go away empty handed. The very last of the peaches that bled he had in the past given to her for her repast. He gave her money instead.

Ever after, he would defy the clown and be himself. Never would he rotate his peaches.

THE KIDS ARE ALL COMIN'

It was unfortunate that Karen had to work the day before Thanksgiving. Flu-like symptoms made a circuit amid her office co-workers. She knew who the malingerers were who were getting a head start to a ski area, calling in sick with artificial coughs. She was office supervisor; and one of her hands would be on her shit list when he returned. Karen could only call with her regrets to her brother, Steve and his wife, Stella.

Vice president, Artie Fowler, hid shadows under his eyes from being up most of the night. Karen covered her shadows with makeup. It was ten o'clock Wednesday evening before she locked her desk and turned out the office lights. She met Artie in the hallway. They walked to their cars together.

"What are your plans?"

"I'll be alone, probably order take-out, watch the Packer game."

"Well, Karen, come over. Have dinner with us. Marion won't mind one more. Let me call her."

"Maybe I will join the two of you, if you're sure. What will you be having, duck or something?"

"More like fourteen for turkey and stuffing. All the kids are comin' this year. You may wind up with a folding chair at the double leaf table. Let's see, four kids, ten grand kids."

"How do you do it, Artie?"

"Marion and I are going away for the weekend......just to sleep!"

THEATRE TICKETS

"Oscar Wilde in person," the poster proclaimed. The photograph portrayed a dashingly handsome male in colorful costume. He would read from "The Importance of being Earnest". His commentary promised to delight audiences everywhere. His sexual orientation preceded him and was widely known. It only served to heighten interest among theatre goers and the "in" crowd.

The reverend Gordon Canby had a reputation of being liberal minded and took in theatre performances with regularity. He would be early in line for his ticket and would be thrilled no end if he could actually meet Oscar Wilde in person back stage.

Having acquired his ticket, row six, seat thirteen at the Orpheum theatre, his mind was accosted by uneasiness. His duties could demand his attention. Emergencies had a way of cropping up at inconvenient times. A death could occur with family to console. What would they think if he showed up later than was expected? He had been seen buying his ticket. People would know where he had been and tongues would wag. His conscience was a harsh taskmaster. He knew his priorities and would succumb, missing the opportunity of a lifetime.

He could not help but show a little nervousness in the two weeks prior to the July eighteenth, 8:00 PM performance. Though, as the time approached, all was quiet. He knew of nothing to interfere with his plans.

Then, the unforeseen happened. He was robbed. A pickpocket made away with his wallet disappearing into the masses. Of course he was embarrassed. Of course he felt undone. Of course something devastating had to deprive him of a pleasure beyond compare!

He stood away, unable to produce his ticket. Tears came to his eyes.

A gentle hand rested on his shoulder.

"I was counting the house and I saw," said a slightly lisping voice. Gordon's eyes met those of the speaker.

He could not believe he was face to face with Oscar Wilde.

"Come, be my guest. I will provide you with a pass."

Elation! Elation! Elation!

DISTURBING CANDLE LIGHT

Madeline Clark, the medallion clerk for the horse show that featured stallions, worked meticulously through the day, and, precisely at 5:00, walked away in the late October darkness toward the lights of Seventh Avenue.

The invitation to the party at the Hall of Mirrors said, "Your presence is requested." She had time and stopped at the Rock Cafe for a light repast. Leaving the cafe, she began to walk east toward the address on the invitation.

A black sedan pulled to the curb. Two men got out, lifted her by her arms and forced her into the back seat. She was stunned. She shrieked until her hands were tied and her eyes blindfolded. She was driven for what seemed an eternity, traveling by turns in many directions. Nervous, head pounding, Madeline tried to listen for voices or anything that would help in a police report if ever she got a chance to file one.

The car stopped. She was carried down a flight of stairs and through a doorway. She was wobbly but could not even faint. Her bonds were loosened and the door slammed behind her. She freed herself and was confronted by darkness lit only by candles in holders on either side of each of many mirrors.

Each mirror she came to seemed to reflect her image grotesquely. Fun mirrors! Except that her appearance altered to show an ever aging countenance. The last mirror reflected a skeletal face. Then lights came on and lit up the room. Her kidnappers were her friends, "friendly persuaders". The exercise had been her initiation. She now had membership in the club that met annually in The Hall of Mirrors of Disturbing Candle light. She would watch in a secret room the initiation of next year's recruit. She would prepare the invitation. She would plan the "escort service" for the male she already had in mind.

The candlelight had provided just the right shadows and the hypnotic suggestion that had scared involuntary scream after scream from her throat.

PRECIOUS CARGO

It was July, 1923, July 10th, 1923, to be exact. Earl Thornberry's mother was dying. He had left Encino, California after graduating from high school. His grades were c's and d's. His outlook on life was to get away, see the country and work for travel money. He worked for a food market manager in Omaha and stayed. East of Missouri remained a dream. He kept in touch with family. In ten years he became manager. Another five years and his third trip home reminded him of how precious his mother had been as his guardian and his tutor and his first love interest. He loved her intensely as a youth, only to disappoint her and vex her in all that she wished for him.

Though he dated and found women interesting, he remained a bachelor in his thirty-fifth year.

His Model A gave him no trouble over the years. He kept it in excellent condition.

Someone was walking along the side of the road near Flagstaff. As he approached, it became clear this was a woman in denim with long blonde hair under a visor. He was wary; and, yet, he was obligated to inquire if she wished a ride. Without hesitation, she put her bedroll in back and climbed in beside him.

This was different. She was different. Her name was Molly Magee. She had traveled by foot and by thumbed rides from Oceanside, New Jersey to visit her sick mother.

Their exchange provided chatter all the way to the California border. He left her where roads diverged in a wood. And he suddenly missed her, almost to tears.

Home. The house, built before the turn of the century, needed paint. The shutters were closed. The neighborhood had seemed quiet with no activity, except for the piston clatter of his car.

The door was locked, but his key still fit. He
entered. No one was there. He called the hospital and
inquired after Margaret Thornberry. She had passed
away that morning.

Earl sat for long hours unmoving, grieving
internally. After three days of arrangements, he buried
his "Mom" next to her estranged husband and prepared
for his return to Omaha.

The miracle of coincidence occurred near the
border with Nevada. Molly was recognizable as the lone
walker, going east.

His heart gave him his cue. He would extend his
time away and finally go east. He would take this
precious cargo all the way home.

They did marry in Oceanside. They did return to
Omaha. They did grow old together. Occasionally, He
would take her to the highway in one direction or another
and let her walk, never letting her out of his sight.

LIGHTS AFTER MIDNIGHT

Grandpa Morgan was lanky and tall. Actually, he was great grandpa to five, ranging from three to ten years old. His thoughts were always on his Heavenly soul mate. They conversed several times a day. His voice carried through the doorway of his room until 9:00 o'clock or so, when he fell asleep.

Grandpa lived with his daughter, Mary and her husband, Carl. Their son, Max, and his wife, Carol, and their two children had moved in with them when his job went away. They all lived together in a get-in-each-other's- way house in Houston.

Grandpa was content with his room and the bathroom until dinner time. He made his way to the table at five-thirty and sat and talked to his Helen. He was eighty-six and wished with all his heart to be eighty sixed and to join her. He felt it was in his power; and yet, there were so many who would miss him, especially Max.

Max, at ten, was a tag-along who saw his grandpa as the greatest fisherman, the greatest companion with whom to ride along. He and his grandpa, then, were joined at the hip. They were still close. Yet, Max wearied of re-told and ever re-told stories by a man who had seen action in the Sicily Campaign and the march on Berlin.

Grandpa had been wounded by shrapnel that left him with a trick knee, a knee that predicted change in the weather. His long life he attributed to clean living, never mentioning his own youthful sins. He met Helen in London while recovering from his war wound. He brought her home as a war bride. He was a self made man whose laundry list of successes and failures could not possibly have occupied the life span of one man. Other incredible events crept into his remembrances as he aged and time seemed to meld his life with those of others he had known.

Family loved and respected Grandpa Morgan; but on many occasions wondered at his voracious appetite for preserving the past.

It was December. What in the world should they give Grandpa for Christmas? At 3:00am on December 7th, Carol got up, went to the bathroom and realized the light was still on in grandpa's room. She woke Max. Together they opened the door. They stood silently watching this grey haired, slender figure on his knees, hands folded, praying—heard his voice praying for release. They panicked when they saw him slump to the floor. Fretting, they woke the others. Carol called 911.

Morgan Chessman was pronounced dead at St. James Hospital at 4:20 am. His Christmas present had come early. Helen had wrapped something special for him.

TOUCHDOWN, NO? SI?

Jerry Hernandez. His Father was of Mexican descent, his mother, German. Marcus Hernandez, whose parents were from Mexico City and legal residents of Denver and the United States owned a produce business and two restaurants. Jerry had a middleclass upbringing in a five room house in a northwest neighborhood. Their new house in Thornton would be ready to occupy in three months time.

November fell slowly toward the holidays which the family observed with wine and festivities.

In September Jerry's cousin, Manual, had come to live with them as an exchange student. Jerry helped him with English, though he had some accented English when he arrived.

They played a verbal game. Jerry would exclaim in a dispute over who was right and who was wrong, "No, see, it's like this; or, he would use it to explain whenever Manual had a question.

They worked hard for money to buy tickets to the Broncos and Packers Thanksgiving Day game at INVESCO Field. Jerry's father would take them.

Into the second quarter the score was tied at ten. The Broncos were driving and on the fifteen yard line of Green Bay. The second down pass was caught in the end zone and touchdown was signaled. Then a late flag was thrown. "Touchdown" Manual yelled. Jerry said, "No!" Manual said, "Si!" Jerry said, "No, see, the play is called back for backfield in motion. They will have to try again. Manual said, "No". Jerry said, "Si, see, they get a five yard penalty. They will get second down over and try again from the twenty yard line". In two plays the Broncos were on the four yard line. Manual said, "First and ten." Jerry said, "No, see, it's first and goal." Manual said, "First and goal, Si."

The Broncos punched the ball in for ...."Touchdown, No?" "Touchdown, Si."

The Broncos won 27—24. Manual said, Broncos are champions, No?" "No, see, they have three more games. They have lost four games. They will not be champions this year."

PARTNERS IN CRIME

A would-be cartoonist sat at his newly acquired drawing board; and there the exercise could have ended. The equivalent of writers block set in as minutes turned into two hours. He mulled the vague notions in his mind, unsatisfied with any premise.

His mice had no "legs". They would not fall into such categories as super mice, flying mice, or mice of heroic might and main. Super mouse had preempted that story line. Mice in conflict with a cat? Done. Mice simply acting humanly? Done. Blind mice? Done. Why mice? He knew he could draw a good mouse. So, he wanted to draw mice.

A thinking cap would have come in handy; but he could only see himself wearing a pointy one made of paper. Suddenly he sang, "Two dunces in a mouse hole." Dunce? Dunces? How about three? Larry, Mo, and Curly. What other names could he use?

Apps, Capps and Frapps were born on a sketchpad, all lines and no color. Apps had overly long ears. Capps had buck teeth and his eyes were crossed. Frapps had a tongue hanging out of his mouth.

Frame after frame went by in strips that had the three distortions of mice engaged in felonious behavior across the house, from stumbling about as they crept and swaggered and wreaked mischief in attempts to get food or frighten members of the household.

When the comic was rejected for the sixth time, the cartoonist became morose and killed his mice, his partners in crime.

He trashed that panel and framed the initial panel; then he sat inert for several hours without a break until a new bulb burned brightly, momentarily, and was lost to fear of failure.

The pesky rooster, Cock-a-doodle-do, filled space in papers everywhere. The strip gave rise to one young man who had quit his job and "bet the farm".

BEYOND THE BEND

Little did Tom Tucker know upon setting out to
hike that he would discover a time warp. "It" took him
away from his familiar landscape. "It" transferred him to
a mountain valley with surface gold glittering in the
sunlight.

His watch had stopped in the moment of the
crossover; time was meaningless in this aberration in the
continuum.

He began walking, convinced this would wear off.
Probably something he ate. He was able to experience
fatigue and sat. He lay out, then slumbered.

Awaking, he found himself surrounded by....
"Lilliputians". He was not confined or restrained. A
shadow stretched out to the left of every individual. He
then noticed his own shadow tapering away to the left.
Simultaneously, the shadows curled up to whisper in
individual ears.

Tom heard, "follow the streambed beyond the
bend." It seemed to have an echo effect as many voices
spoke as one. "Slay the monsters and claim your
kingship and its vast lands and wealth." Tom shook his
head; but all was the same as before. He began to doubt
that this was not reality, that he had somehow become
lost in a somewhere that actually existed. He might as
well play the game, take them at their word, and have a
Sinbad-like adventure to tell..... if he ever got his life
back.

His mind calculated three miles to the bend. He
could reach it in less than an hour. Yet, no matter how
much ground he covered, the bend always seemed the
same distance away. His companions seemed willing to
accompany him to the bend. They had to skip and run to
catch up with his stride. No more shadow curl. No more
communication.

Was he on an invisible treadmill? Where was he caught, in his own mind? How could he ever reach the bend and the land of monsters beyond the bend?

Then another voice whispered, "fly". Ha! He leapt into the air, expecting a harsh landing. Yet, he was able to fly around the bend to where the golden sword awaited. Time no longer stood still. The monsters were grotesque yet appeased, docile, and not a bit scary.

"Tom, what were you doing wandering the grounds by yourself? How did you leave without detection and without an attendant? I understand you speared a woodchuck with a sharpened stick. Can you tell me anything?" Jenna Spear waited for a response. When Tom sat silently mumbling to himself, she made a notation for a special watch to be put on him and to have his medication evaluated.

Tom knew where he had been. He did not remember how he got home to his room at Grace Sanatorium. He knew he had gone around the bend, only vaguely knowing when.

CHESTER'S CHOICE

Chester Washington was caught in the dilemma of having to choose. He could not have both a guitar and a keyboard for Christmas. His parents promised one if he could decide which. That was in mid November.

He was troubled for weeks, tossing and turning in bed and being awake when he should have been sleeping peacefully. Money was not a problem; and he was sure both would not be a serious imposition on a budget that gave him ten dollars a week for allowance. At least in his

mind it seemed rational and without merit that he
should have to do without one or the other.

He went about telling friends that it must be
punishment for something. The more he made his
feelings known, the more he was sure he had hit on the
reason. He would take any other punishment if he would
not have to pay for this transgression on Christmas Day.

One day he screwed up his courage and
approached his parents with his concern. He asked what
he had done and gave them assurance they could do
whatever else they thought appropriate. Both parents
were surprised and taken aback. It never occurred to
them he would feel he had done something wrong.

His mother said, "No, you don't understand.
Whichever you choose, we want to get the very best there
is; and we want you to practice it to the exclusion
of the other until you have mastered it. With dedication
you can someday have both."

Ponder time came calling with its bag of tricks,
pulling Chester one way then the other. He thought of
world tours, playing classical guitar. He could have
recognition with keyboard and lead singer in a rock band.
Both thoughts gave him equal pleasure while he
contemplated them.

Let his friends decide! Let the choice be theirs!
Unfortunately they were equally divided in their
opinions. He was stuck, after all with having to choose
one or neither. His fingers began to drum. Buddy Rich
came to mind. Elated, he was almost persuaded to
switch altogether.

"It's time, Chester. You must decide today", his
father said at breakfast. "Tell us at dinner tonight."
Silently he thumbed his nose at the prospect. To his
wide-eyed amazement the choice had been made. So
many to emulate, learn from, or be inspired
by—Satchmo, Doc Severnson, Dizzy Gillespie, Winton
Marsalis.

"Have you decided?"

"Yes, I should like the very best trumpet there is."

What shone under the tree was just that.

THE DELL FARM

Pastoral, with silent passiveness, but activity, the Dell Farm hung quietly in unobtrusiveness. The Dell Farm was in a dell, surrounded by rolling hills that created an uneven horizon. The farm house was surrounded by cottonwoods. Landscaping included fences and a dairy barn. No cows were visible. One had the impression they would become visible at any moment. Farmhands with buckets were entering the barn. A border collie trotted with lively business-like demeanor. Gamecocks hung by the barn door.

The painting was for sale, April 17, 1842, in a London gallery. The viewer could not afford it.

SUZY, PLAIN AND SIMPLE

It was as though she had a target on her back. She was often the object of whispering by those who delighted in a tsking moment. "The grace of God was sometimes used as a humanitarian gesture when guilt plagued the observer of the plain and simple Suzy Wellman.

She looked in the mirror without a critical eye toward her appearance. She took herself for granted and presented a laugh-like smile, open mouthed and genuine, as if she could not help it. She bathed herself; she dressed herself; she followed her daily regimen without being prompted. She greeted people lovingly; and she prayed. In her world nothing was complicated.

Family loved her, and accepted her limitations only if she proved unable to go beyond them.

Pillar to post and trial and error were a part of her existence from the age of three until her chronological age of twelve. Beyond twelve those who worked with her held little hope for progress.

Gradually she changed to grown up in body and features and complexion and dexterity. She looked in the mirror on her 18th birthday in her new birthday dress and makeup. (Mom still helped her with that.) Mom stood beside her. "You're beautiful", Mom said.

"That is beautiful", Suzy said matter-of-factly. "And I'm beautiful here." Her right forefinger was pointing at her heart.

WINTER WALTZ

Charles Martinez talked to the winter weather and the scene before him. He expected no reply but that which came to him as elements of weather, setting, sounds and visual perceptions. He was grounded in science, which interfered with a poet's eye. He was of two conflicting worlds. Everything was broken down for him into its components. His science mind did not object. But his things-of-the spirit mind personified everything that surrounded him. The poet talked with thy, thee and thou and addressed the rink and trees and the warming shack and the ice upon the rink and the clouds and the sky and all living things, great and small.

His mind would say, "Tree, come, dance with me. I would have a partner this day. Thy tresses fascinate me. Thou art a filter for the sun. Why are you not leafless this time of year?"

"I am red and gold. Leaves will soon fall with the advent of winter."

"Ice, a waltz upon thee would be good for my soul."

"I am as yet too fragile. But imagine we are as one in great swings and whirls."

"Clouds, when shall I find the dark and slated, to bring cold and snow, below zero temperatures pervading the region—those that would make a statue of a waltzing figure?"

"All form a circle. Let us dance together; one, two, three; one, two, three; one, two, three."

Science, "I don't get it."

Poet's muse, "Beauty is truth, truth beauty", quoting Keats beautifully.

A GOOD TIME FOR PATIENCE

"Damned Astroturf! Never liked the looks of it. We played on the real stuff, mud holes and all. Didn't get a damn million dollars to play, or even fifty dollars. We played for thirty dollars a game and five dollars meal money. Them days there want no fancy pads or helmets. Holler and hand signals to rely on··· and patience."

Old Doc Poston was a graduate of the ramblin' wreck school. He started a football career in the instructional league and after a couple of years washed out. He always thought he could make the big time if he worked hard enough and long enough. Every year he applied for another chance in patient trust that an opening would show and he could resume his climb. "Sorry" was his only reward.

The trouble was he wasn't fast enough. Never would be. His times were half a second off. His timing was off in hitting the hole. He took uppers occasionally, but the come-down left him a step away from his chance at glory. He was doggedly patient, certain that his hard work would pay off.

It never did. His release was final. No one wanted him. Even at forty-four he persisted in a training regimen. It was never a time for "quit". He told himself there was no quit in him.

Now, at eighty-five was a good time for patience. His mind was sharp. He could teach a thing or two to the boys on the field.

CASINO CASUALS

He was twenty-one today and legal. He was fulfilling his wish, something for which he had saved for two years. He would spend the night playing 21. Flopping cards and breaks would ensue until three in the morning or until he was broke. That would be ok. The object of the exercise would be to imitate the wheelers and dealers being played out on the big screen. The casual look of high rollers, he would feel in himself on his evening out.

He dialed up "Luck, Be a Lady Tonight" and called a cab at 5:00. He would dine alone and drift to a table, in time, casually. Perhaps a companion would find him, though he would not seek out a distraction. He, Vince Vittroelli, might save out enough to buy one and a nightcap.

Betty Warren eyed the baby-faced young man who was winning big, if she could count cards, and she could. She could be patient. She moved to the entrance and looked out at the street and the traffic and the pedestrians and those who came and went.

Back to business had her eyes glued to one who seemed he could not loose, at least not more than a hand in ten. The eyes on the monitor watched, too. This was a run that would end. They all did.

At 2:00 o'clock Betty made a move. Behind him, she ran a finger against the grain across the hairs on his neckline.

"Maybe you could cash in and we could go to my place, your room if you like." She was whispering with a breathless quality in her voice.

Not looking up, Vince said, "This soldier has another hour to go. Go back and sit down. Now!" Betty was taken aback but returned quietly to her seat and waited.

At three he cashed for twenty thousand dollars. Betty followed, took his arm, and whispered, "I'm ready." Casually, he said, "Frankly, my dear, I don't give a damn!" And he left alone. She was too old for him.

HANDOUT WITH STRINGS

Tito's Italian was closed. It was scrubbed and polished and ready for business. But, it was closed. A one day closing had been advertised for March, 21st, a month prior to the event

Tito was an immigrant from the old country. He worked twenty years to own his place. The early hard times and the handouts he received made him appreciate what could happen in America. On many occasions he felt hopelessly unable to get ahead, working long hours for others. He had a Tevi urge to plead with God. He did not have to be rich, just satisfied that he had made it.

At ten am, Tito placed the sign in the door. "By Invitation Only", it read. Those who had been given invitations would arrive at various times throughout the day and evening, at their convenience. They would present the doorman with a free meal certificate for whatever was on the menu. As many as 100 people would come through the door. That many invitations had been given out personally by "the boss".

Three violins played. Tito sang joyfully to the customers as they came and went, filled with meals they never before had tasted, served with garlic bread, and polished off with dessert. Wine bottles were left at the tables.

The clientele that day were street people.

PEOPLED IN GLORIOUS

Their garments were of no consequence. They did cover, however, the whatever clothes people brought with them. Colors were pastels to be absorbed by free minds with a disposition to like pastels; cool for minds that were cool; cold for minds pristine and unattached to others; warm for those who took on warm thoughts to distribute. There were no clashing symbols warranting opposition.

Views were not, therefore not opposing. Only were reflections carried of carnal habitations and all the detritus it entailed. "Not" was belied by this coexistence beyond what lay in state.

All illusions to identity faded with the transformation. The greeted one requited love with love and took joy with it in its passage to the Kingdom. It bowed in courtesy to warm and cool and cold alike and did honor to the highest presence in wholehearted trust.

Cool and cold were still on a journey and could not comprehend their state; and yet, they were arrayed in glorious and eternally at peace.

THE GIST OF THE TEXT

Herman Goble was fifteen. He went to the Synagogue to study the text of the words of the law and the prophets. Past his Bar Mitzvah, he had a burning desire to understand everything. He would become a Rabbi and teach out of his understanding. He thought of it as a calling, lifelong and noble.

The shelves of books available to him looked inviting but formidable. Tucked in the H's was one with soft leather binding; and gold leaf letters on the spine read Holy Bible. He took this heavy volume from the shelf and studied its contents. It contained the books of the law and the prophets in the Old Testament. For the first time he discovered the Christian books of the New Testament. He wondered why this book took a place with all the others. He would have to ask Rabbi Rosenthal. If the Bible was within his reach, it must have value for him. Herman turned to the New Testament, interested but leery of being influenced by it. Was he not compromising his study time? He felt somehow he was cheating on his commitment.

Yet, the gospels seemed, in the gist of the text, to present a "son of God" among men who must fulfill the need of God to have this son die as a means of man's salvation. He had followers, even beyond his death, committed far more intensely than he, to keep alive the story.

Strangely, the words of the man, Jesus, were that he came to fulfill the law and spoke of the one great commandment that "ye love one another."

One day the Rabbi found Herman reading the book and sat quietly. When Herman closed the book, Rabbi Rosenthal said in low tones, "You are not reading history only but mythology. It contains a spiritual truth for all of your days. It, too, should give you comfort in your journey. Life eternal has many shades of meaning. Resolve it for yourself and find contentment."

Herman rose and put his hand on the elderly man's shoulder. "Thank you", he said and returned to the books that interpreted the laws.

MERCIES UNDONE

James Priestly came to the hobo camp with the intention of being a thief in sheep's clothing. He was a most friendly fellow who could easily earn trust. He took the time to entrench himself in the minds of others as one who was earnestly good and willing to be of help. A source of information of what services were where and what valuable items were worth, he became popular with all those who had "finds" or items they would part with for cash.

He would have no hurry in him. He would lift things over time with varied intervals, immediately selling the items and banking the cash. He would force a Samaritan way for the good of all.

Over the years, when James needed hernia repair, it was paid for. When Jennifer got cancer, she was helped. When Ollie broke his leg, crutches were bought. Always anonymous donors gave James cash to distribute, or so he told them.

On the seventh day of the ninth month of the twelfth year his mercies ended. He was caught by Jack, as in lumberjack, taking Birdie's new necklace. James died from a brutal beating in an alley off Larimer Street.

TWO SCRIBBLE-ISTS

Dueling critics can make for delightful entertainment. It is not certain, however, that no disservice to readers is accomplished inadvertently. The energy involved in that endeavor might better be expended in the reviews each creates.

It is not certain who began the sniping exchanges that Joey Parsons of the Tribune and Mark Chase of the rival Morning Sun carried on over the lives of their columns. It was only certain that those exchanges improved the circulation numbers for each of the papers. Thus, they were encouraged. Editors even made suggestions in bull sessions with their respective reporters.

Pens (computers) mightier than the sword crossed from a distance of fifty thousand paces—the distance between the two papers.

Joey was seventy five, when eighty was around the corner for Mark, seventy nine. Mark wrote of this occasion that would "mark" his birthday with a mock "aw shucks". Though, the two of them seldom crossed paths and were coldly civil toward each other when they were forced into the same venues. None-the-less Mark declared it an act of charity and extended an invitation to Joey to attend the buffet at Maxies'. He then put aside his column to think up Joey jokes with which he intended to embarrass his avowed opponent. Disappointment would reign if Joey declined.

It was too good an opportunity for Joey. Occasionally, he would put his column aside to think up jokes to embarrass the old fart in front of his honored guests. Think of the names of those who would be there! Think of the material they would give each other for future columns!

But, none of that took place. The evening before
the big event Mark collapsed and was rushed to the
hospital. He had suffered a major heart attack. He was
kept alive for three days before he passed away.

Joey's heart melted and his column was a birthday
eulogy, glowing in its assessment of a Mark Twain wit
and a larger than life persona.

Now he would have to find a new someone he could
love to hate.

CHICKEN SALAD

Bessie May Barnes inevitably showed up at a funeral reception with her unique recipe of chicken salad. The salad was wolfed down by those who came because of it. Bessie's ego was satisfied no end as she watched it disappear. Young men who were obligated to attend by parents lined up for sandwiches, chicken salad and dessert.

At the commemoration of the life of Beulah Graves, a stranger named Angela Davis came and was welcomed. Her dish, covered and in a shiny bowl, was set in the middle of the buffet tables, which were set up end to end and wore fresh linen. At the hour of one PM, the dishes were uncovered to reveal their contents. And, what to the wandering eyes should appear but two bowls of salad, with chicken, it was clear. Bessie's chicken was baked and golden brown. Large strips were succulent with crispy coating and generously applied to the rest of the ingredients; lettuce, tomatoes, bacon, olives, parmesan and Caesar Dressing. Angela's chicken was boneless, skinless, and looked dry. It seemed sparse as well.

At three o'clock, Bessie's bowl was empty and scrapings showed the diligence with which every bit had been devoured. Angela's salad went largely untouched. It filled leftover cartons to be taken home.

Bessie went to Angela, who seemed to have a tear in her eye. "Come," she said, "I will give you my recipe."

FARM OASIS

It was called the Craig Sanders Farm. Actually, it was an orchard. Its major crop was peaches. Craig Sanders was not a religious man. Others' Sabbath was another work day for him and for his family. He had no quarrel with farm hands or pickers who attended services or Mass. It was only imperative that work get done. They could work in shifts if it were critical that crops were harvested on time and packed and shipped.

Everyone got extra from the tithe he exacted from his own earnings. Half was kept in reserve to aid one who stopped for help. Word got around and as time went on, he found something to feed someone or take on an unneeded hand for a day more and more frequently. His earnings and his tithe seemed to grow exponentially with the greater need.

He was able to expand his acreage and diversify his crops. His wealth allowed for the education of his children...he did not expect any to follow in his footsteps. They were free to pursue their own interests.

In his seventy-seventh year all of the kids had gone off to be a lawyer, a dentist, a singer and a teacher. When he died, all flew in to attend the funeral and to comfort their mother. Each expected to inherit something.

It seemed natural that Craig's way of doing business would end with him. They never expected Judith, his young widow, to inherit everything and to carry on his traditional oasis farm and its tithe.

PASTORAL WITH KANGAROO

Midnight, and the museum was dimly lit and deserted. Security alarms were on. Quiet hung like invisible fog on the surrounding landscape. The new exhibition would open the following day; throngs were sure to attend the ticketed display of the Danish artist, Lon Borg.

Some notoriety made him a controversial figure. Critics were lavish with both praise and condemnation. He was called both genius and fraud. To some extent he was attracted to the attention and was prone to overstate the representations he invested in his pieces. He was believed to have enameled feces and glued them to panel board; though no one ever saw it displayed.

Moth and rust were kept at bay. But that night, thieves did break in and steal a veritable show piece that had been heralded by all the critics as a masterpiece. Entitled "Pastoral with Kangaroo", it engaged the eye almost hypnotically. An enlarged landscape held a very small and insignificantly placed figure wearing boxing gloves.

The painting was not recovered for forty-four years until it turned up in an out of the way venue in upstate New York, which was attended by word-of-mouth recipients.

Lon Borg, now eighty-five, was informed by the museum's representative. Police recovered the painting. Lon kept it in a vault until his death. When his estate was auctioned, the painting stayed in the vault.

THE ANDERSON BRIGADE

It began with an attack of wearisome fatigue. Major Ronald Anderson had been awake with insomnia for three days, dozing fitfully a few minutes at a time, but infrequently. He went to the infirmary and was subsequently hospitalized for observation and treatment.

Having been found in good health, he was given a strong sedative and allowed to rest undisturbed. His office was informed and Colonel Remark filled in for him. Now, something more than sleep had found him. His no! no! no! was not heard, for it was only in his mind at the close of a very real and terrifying nightmare.

The Anderson Brigade had the left flank during a fire fight. The Germans many times overran his positioned troops, slaughtering without mercy and without ceasing. His mind roved back and forth for several hours in extreme anguish. The sedative only heightened the anguish in intense sleep. The Germans went on to conquer Paris, London, and all of Western Europe; and it was his fault. He could have done no other than what he did, thin the lines to the sea.

Wrestling with an angel would have been a welcome diversion. He was an exhausted wreck, unable to speak the first day of his confinement.

After three days, he learned of Allied victories and German defeats. Armistice Day prevented another cold day in Hell.

MAGNIFICENT SOB SESSION

A sign with an arrow read, "Up one flight, to the right, please to ring the bell, DR. BLAZON, DDSPHD. A dentist liked to draw out his patients. His was a jovial face and demeanor that put at ease the busy, the nervous, those in pain, or those who were somehow afflicted with sadness.

"Anything troubling you?" he asked. Gloria responded with glistening tears that wet her eyes with new sparkle. Her mouth retreated to a down turn and her lips quivered.

"I've been so close to my Auntie May. She's gone now. I miss her a lot. She kept us all laughing, enjoying life." Her voice cracked. Sobs convulsed her. She wept openly.

Dr. Benjamin Blazon patted her arm. "Would you like to re-schedule? No extra charge. Perhaps you should wait a few days, maybe a week. I could fit you in."

Gloria continued to sob openly, loudly, and with much use of tissue.

Finally she calmed and quietly submitted to having a permanent cap put in place. Outside, she called her director and said, "That went well. My Aunt May should have heard me carry on. It would have been a real hoot for her. I'm ready for tomorrow's shoot.

BARNEY STOPPED RUNNING

January! And the cardboard barely kept the wind chill factor above freezing. Home was a compressed paper shelter for Barney Mcgoogleyes. This chapped, weather beaten, scrawny old man of forty-five came to Denver with a broken past hard on his heels. He needed a place to rest and answer all the questions that tormented his mind.

The stock show was in full swing. He could look off in the distance and see the throng arriving by car, bus, and even limousine. He would go and get warm! A past master at the art of the fast shuffle, he would mingle with the wave that moved slowly toward the arena entrance.

He would make his way forcefully to the fence, touching stock with a familiar hand. He would ask directions to the stock entrance. He would leave and return again, having made a show of leaving. Later, he would walk right in the stock show entrance unchallenged with several others as judging time neared. Any dark corner would do, then.

Back in the box for the night, Barney grew hair and was warm. He could not have survived in human form.

POEMS

DAWNS ANEW

The dawn comes up then goes away.
The day is fine—
Until the news that someone died.
The breath attached to family ceased.
And the one bereft has cried.

Wounded is another way of tasting
What is of sour bred
And has the name of (sadly) Sorrow's bread.
But, then, some joy is reached
In many dawns ahead.

SCARLET IN GLORIOUS DEFEAT

I watched the twilight
Do magic with the sky.
The paint box spilled.
The various shades of grey of clouds;
And brilliant edges formed
As red ran off toward west
And faded into that lavender
The lessening light enhanced.
Suddenly black proclaimed a victory.
I mourned the passing of the sun,
As it declaimed its valedictory.

SLIPS OF LAVENDER

Oops! The red has gone lavender
In early morning grey.
Slips of lavender greet a new day, dawning.
Light behind a strip of redness
Gathers in intensity;
And a voice inside me stresses,
"Let it be! Let it be!
But, not the voice of deep regret,
Nor song of deep remorse,
Nor song of fading darkness
When lavender slips away.

OLD MAN'S REVERIES

He sits alone
In his place
In his park
In his corner
Of the world.

Only a blink
Reveals
His wakefulness
Fully warmed
By afternoon
Sun.

He wears a hat.
He slumps slightly
Sideways
To the right.
His left arm presses
The top of the back
Of the bench
Tightly.

Eighty if a day
He has nothing
To say
That muttering
Wont accomplish.

He lost his wife.
He's going blind.
He somehow
Wants to find
His daughter.
He looks across
The lakefull water
And repeats himself.

He gets up slowly,
Head's bowed lowly,
Hands on knees.
He'll catch tomorrow
Once again
His reveries.

MAMA SINGING

In focus, out again, sat aging Mama.
A veteran of caring sat holding her hands.
A tidy room, spare, displaying remembrances,
Was warmly cozy about them.
An hour's ride brought her daughter to her side
To help them sing.
Words came to Mama "in focus".

For now, light falls were concerns;
But she was safe for now.
Mama, frail against the Mama of years past
Could put melody in her voice,
 Though not always by choice.
Words came out of long ago.

Picture Mama's last song, a hymn.
Picture Mama singing.
Visualize a low alto, fading.
Picture Mama's dance through life.

LETTING GO

It is a brave thing to do
To let someone go who
Has been loved.
It is a brave thing to do
To stand bowed and weep—
Unashamedly—
Over the no-going-back.
Once is all there is except
For emotions re-collected
From a time remembered.
You are the rock now
That the loved one once was.
And, Life has dominion in
The newness of a beginning.

BOTH SIDES NOW

She is gone now.
It was she who took thrifty to heart.
Sayings passed down from long ago
Gave her daughter the lessons to follow.

"A penny saved is a penny earned.
Take bargains to heart,
Be thrifty and save and don't fill the cart.
Only take care of your needs", Mother said.

Recipes came down, passed on through generations.
She learned cooking and passed it on.
Her daughter remembers her pot roast, her casseroles,
her pies.
Her daughter remembers the thrift in her eyes,
The look she has given her own daughter.

THE REMEMBRANCE TREE

It had age on it when I ran to it,
Affected by its patient stand.
Umbrella'd leaves made shade.
I cooled to shuddering.

I wandered down a memory lane of boxcars on a train;
And standing there, I felt the pain of "gone".
The memory tree seemed to know,
As if its limbs were sawn.

Railcar after railcar carried scenes of poor, sad faces,
Happy gleefulness,
School and rigid quietness
And yells of joy and "fight!" at recess:
Carried scenes of passing on through olderness and
change.
(The tasting of the plentiful would never cease.
And the body, over time, became obese.)

Remembered good, remembered kindness, remembered
love and sorrow,
And newness ever of tomorrow and tomorrow and
tomorrow
Lighted lane with embered flame
To mark each passing year.

The tree whispered, "The caboose is gone beyond horizon
limitation.
Let go, let go, let go."

I touched tree bark at close to dark.
I bowed my thanks for remembrance.
I left, for bed to sleep, to work, to play, to wed the new.
And the remembrance tree, I knew, would wait for me.

DOWN BY THE LEVI

The old lady got her feet wet up to her eyebrows.
And her tens of thousands fled for their very lives.
Much disquiet discussed the wherefores and the whys
and hows
To the tune of row, row, row your boat toward one who
survives.
From destructive hurricane's deadly path
Came a dirty, toxic bath,
A witch's cauldron—
A devil's brew—
And its consequence of wrath.
Old Lady, have you not yet drowned? Will there yet be a
second time around? Will your bustle be a thing to
admire? New fame perhaps you will acquire.
You were fabled for jazz—
 Hirt, Fountain, bands with pzazz.
 All have been tabled for a duration While gods have been
appeased
With oblation.
Strike up a parade for the Old Lady's passing.
Make way for the thousands in the New Lady, amassing.

THE OLD CLOWN

Often called, "Old Crone", now,
The wizened woman remembered the clown
Who was nimble and on her way
Into children's hearts to stay.

Embittered. Time had robbed her
Of sleight of hand that would occur,
To open-mouthed amazement,
To fool the way the gaze went
And suddenly produce surprise.

The young clown she was tries
To come forth again when
She relives in poke-a-dots
And a face covered in spots
Days when her career was practiced and assured
And any thoughts of being cast aside were absurd.

Steadied by a wooden cane, too,
The mirrored image bent and stumbled anew,
Or could not find the chain of silks
To bring out endlessly knotted together.
The tears by a wart covered nose
Were reflections of emotion that arose
In lonely reflection upon the haggard pose
That, today, was the unkindest cut of all.

She could no longer stand erect and tall.
She could only wish for a magic fountain of youth,
Cry because she could not move a mountain of truth
Or even die.

TRANSPOSED

She of the broad persuasion and broad disposition
Defined her life in terms of a broad's profession.
She of the soft curls and soft curves and soft skin
Spoke softly without some conscious thought of sin.
Parading her traffic in evening's chill, immodest dress,
Blondie, in her forties, coughed on a regular basis
As her cigarette smoking gave her eights and aces.

There was no quit in her as she smoked and trolled
And smiled sincerely toward lookers who were bold.
She hooked some johns in random, unordered, selection.
Though she knew how to treat them and take direction.

Her life now was not all she had ever possessed.
Her life had been encased in loving family, blessed.
She had given herself as a bride of Christ then reneged;
Then in guilt and disharmony forgiveness begged.

She had married. She had given birth. She was content.
She certainly believed her children had been heaven-
sent.
She looked forward to her unhurried days of peaceful
quiet.
She even looked forward to lettuce in her slimming diet.

Blondie, Jenny McGrath, suddenly took to an ugly path,
As she did a Madame Bovary and walked away in wrath
Brought on by "salt" put into wounds by uncaring others,
Husband, in-laws, children, friends, sisters, brothers.

Transposed in a dream ungodly real, she loudly
screamed.
The house came alive; and into her room her family
streamed.
Now she was grey; now she was widowed, now mixed up.
But, she was still grandma! Her "love" life was again
fixed up.

THAT STEP OF TRUST

Out under a sky that threatens, undeterred,
One of a multitude of life forms breathes quickly.
That one considers the weather and is conflicted by it.
That one is indecisive and must take that step of trust
Ingrained in one whose mission lies into the elements.

Out under a sky of placid illumination, stirred,
The result of coital explosion picks up a scent of danger
And hesitates, wondering whether to fear the elements
Or to venture forth and take a commission as a leader
In strained reply to terrible things the Lord hath
wrought.

One can take that step of trust and succeed or fail,
But only as one meant to assail the thunderous perils
Accosting beings, from every side, who ride the storm.
Rather, in spite of all, tempered by rational belief,
One has no other trial than death to reach a noble goal.

LITTLE PIECES

ALPHA BET

Two existed before light and matter.
They played mental games,
Transferring thought to each other.
One controlled mass and might
While mighty mite controlled microscopic.
The greater had pure vision.
The sight of the lesser was myopic.

The urge for competition brought father and son to a
contest.
"Mine' will be bigger than yours, son".
"Can you do it without mine?"
Space filled with flash-bang and tremendous uproar,
With collisions and explosions and awesomeness.
The Cosmos was all over atom sprayed.
"Told you," the son said.

EX-WISEY

For his knowledge and intelligence the elderly
gentleman was called Wisey. He gave freely of his
wisdom and his years.   His was the word of wisdom and
restraint. His was a lesson in apology to save others'
feelings. Wisey would step in to salvage what would
otherwise be rent in anger. Everyone blessed him as a
peacemaker.

The unthinkable happened on a rainy Sunday.
Wisey died. According To his wishes his tombstone was
engraved with the words, "HERE LIES EX WISEY.

GETTING THE NOD

Polished politician promotes himself—
His platform is the statehouse steps.
A Gargoyle head spews words.
He uses buzz words with plenty of reps.

 Polished politician promotes discord.
To get the nod to get elected
To be the one who is selected
To be the one, when all is said and done,
To be in past times recollected
Or in present times resurrected
To be the one to get elected.

TEDIOUS AFTERWARD

Flat. And unable to move this or that
Or. Even feel another's touch.
The mind can only go after so many radii.
And. Those whose lives are peripheral,
Packing other venues including stadia,
Become boring.
The mortar shell's impact knocked him
Flat. Unable to move this or that.
"I'm gone! Forgive me, for I have sinned."
Uttering epithets had slowly thinned
Within. He was chagrinned
To discover unimagined tedious
Afterward.

THE MUSIC SITTER

Mind the music and the step....
The Music Sitter, full of pep,
Propelled herself toward fame
By tending to "All in the Game,"
"The Hills Are Alive with sound,"
"Peace in the Valley" round.
The Muse of music marched in tune
To various and sundry croon
 And spoon and moon of songs
Dedicated to the right of wrongs,
To love and broken-heartedness
And lost in wonder and wilderness,
Whatever melodiously conspired
To test some emotionally bronze-fired
Configurations and produce relationships
Of stories and sing of glories and
Defeats.

PASSENGER X

A figure with no name rode in a corner seat, quietly, unobtrusively and dressed in black. His mission was to silence another in death. He was a silent partner with life as it passed into no-breath.

Well suited to his task, he stared straight ahead. His only thought was of the dead-to-be riding with a folded umbrella. He had materialized as the train sped and Mary Etheridge's ticket had been punched as she went into fibrillation. Mary was saved. Passenger X disappeared. Her reservation was rescheduled. Ten years after Mary was saved Mary was saved at an eleventh hour; and the Death Angel had his way.

THE POSE

James Andrews, with head bandaged and crutches supporting him, stood in profile. Sara Blige faced him holding his hands. Her right leg wore a prosthetic. Sara smiled at a picture of pain and would take half of it if she could. They were at the beach and should be looking at the ocean. But they would not. She would not give herself joy when he could not share it. She found her joy in their pose for a photographer who would illustrate their story.

Both were fragmentation victims and met on the long flight home. They rehabbed together and married seven months from the day they were wounded.

PRAY AND PRAISE

Why should I reach back and bring forth teachers?
Why should a demanding God strut before the crestfallen
rich
Except to say, "Use two words to touch the poor in Spirit,
Pray and praise for bounty for the do·with·outs?
Don't separate your ways from my ways".

YELLOW TAIL

Not only for show and not only for neatness
The braid fell seventeen inches into a tie·up.
It was tight, flaxen, resplendent with ribbon—
Blue ribbon for a blue·ribbon braid.
One shoulder or the other nestled a rope of hair,
While a smile that was thin and spare
Touched the men in the room with delight.
Taught to curl and touch a cheek
As her neck was kissed by warm lips,
Helen's yellow tail put flame in her flirting.
After all, who really was she hurting?
She could unfold a fan and create distance,
A zone of safety while making herself desirable,
Mysterious, able to take yellow·tailed flight.

ZEAL UNDER DURESS

Partly hardy, unable to confess,
Zealots come forth to address
Pain inflicted by the powerfully unrestrained.
Patiently crying, subservience feigned,
Zealots endure, with Heaven secure,
The absence of what they could have gained.
"Praise the Lord and pass the ammunition.
If your hand offends you, cut it off.
Or I will help."
Thus says the Zealot with a machete.
"Fear the Lord and get hammered.
Be a miracle worker and get hammered.
God will take care of you if you are enamored
Of getting hammered in God's name."
Thus spake Zealot-thustra.

HUMOR DOOR

Open the door and see all the smiles.

SPITTIN' POLLACKS

Spittin' Pollacks: Sittin' around spittin', tryin' to put spit
in a spittoon,
Spitters are spittin' tobacco juice
All over a tile floor.
Artistic stainin' is allowed today;
And, Jackson Pollack would be proud of what is wrought
As tobacco stain begins to clot.
The lesson is, I am told, that, tobacco should be spat, not
rolled.

DOGGIE TWEETS

Back and forth between man and dog
Hand signals and responses flash within the space of
seconds
Over, bark, over, bark, bark, over, bark, bark, bark—
One, two, three, nice and neat.
Man to dog, dog to man, tweet, tweet, tweet.
Cell phone on, he hears his master's voice.
Bark, bark, bark; he doesn't have a choice.
They tweet; they tweet; they tweet, tweet, tweet.

THE CZECH IS INTO MAIL

The Czech is proud to be asked, when a gathering takes place. There are weddings and parties and gala dances and backyard feasts and family dinners, at extended tables, replete with a variety of meats and plenty of potatoes and rutabagas or turnips. Three pies loosen belts to make room.

The Czech waits patiently for the postal person, expecting a new invitation to be delivered. The formal request of one's presence is always the traditional means of saying, "Come on over." And, the Czech is into mail.

CHESTER'S UNDERWEAR

As a child in the nineteen fifties, Chester Newman learned Morse code and Semi-fore. One could send away for them with a few box tops and twenty-five cents.

Chester, the bird watcher and outdoor enthusiast, on occasion would be better served to capture himself with a butterfly net. He did not always think of being cautious. Of a Sunday in field gear and binoculars hung around his neck he set forth. At mid morning he crossed shallow water to an island some thirty yards from shore.

At 3:05 PM a deluge ensued from the sky and created a torrential rush of water through the channel that had earlier been a trickle. Convinced he would be washed away, Chester felt he needed rescuing. He cut a limb with his trusty knife's saw blade. Then he removed his trousers and his shorts. Having reclaimed his modesty by putting on his trousers, he placed his underwear on the pole and raised it high. Not exactly semi-fore, it did affect his rescue and invited notoriety from the Media.

FATHER AND SON

Together counts for something,
At least to the father,
When a backyard fence needs repair.
Of a morning, the two would gather
In the early light
To wall out the neighbor's dog with its continual bark
and stare.
Expert son needed no one to aid him
In replacing a worn out post.
It was the father who needed the together experience the
most.

"I got it, Dad," to a staggering elder
Placed them in separate categories of age and experience
and fitness.
It was the son who did the heavy lifting;
While the father was a prideful witness.

LITTLE WHIRLWIND DANCE

I watched a flying insect
Attack a moth upon the ground.
Engaged, the two did whirl around
Until there was disengagement.
Attack began anew, setting up a whirl
In which the two did twirl and twirl and twirl.
Perhaps it was a game to the flyer;
Perhaps it satisfied the desire
To engage in sport of a deadly sort
To prove itself superior
As the moth grew wearier and wearier.
The throes of death, a curious thing,
Produced the thought, "O Death,
There is thy sting."

THANKS TO DARWIN

Folks were quite content with the story of the Ark that saved the world. The story did a good job of explaining a new beginning that had the purpose of delighting God's children and gave a reality test to a widely circulated notion of floods that could wipe out all living things.

Publication of facts clung dearly to memories and embellishments grounded in the supernatural. Miracles gave God credibility and the ensuing story of man's fall and redemption carried forward.

Thanks to Darwin Many minds turned away from a God of the universe in a loving relationship with His creation and him who was a little less than the Angels. Poof! No more God. A monkey's uncle seemed to be an adequate replacement. And, the no-God-ers studied the creatures of nature, satisfied with themselves. Women of science joined their quest.

Thanks to Darwin, "Save the species" became the battle cry for mankind, butterfly collections notwithstanding.

CHIPPER'S PARADISE

There were twelve men and one woman who called themselves chippers. They were artists who chipped away at logs in the backwoods of upper Michigan. Logging provided them with material for their axes and chisels and carving knives. Their intricate carvings sold for hundreds, even thousands of dollars.

But civilization encroached. Thirteen woodcarvers constantly fought authorities who found them to be a hindrance to progress.

They lived together in twos and threes, and, as in the case of Maria Long Feather, alone. Their camps were unkempt and deemed hazards. They slept in sleeping bags in tents. They were perpetual campers who constantly had to move their sites. Eventually they packed up and disappeared from the region. Only their customers missed them.

They reappeared across the border. The French Canadians appreciated their artistry and ceded seven square miles as a sanctuary. Maria Long Feather found herself in an "island paradise" that had all the material she could use in a lifetime. Her French became impeccable. Her legacy was her works and her young protégé.

August 25th, 1975, Maria Long Feather was buried between two statuary works in "Paradise".

ARBOR CONVERSATION

There were Matt and Mattie, two individuals so disparate in their views and dispositions they met once a day to argue and take the measure of a good day by the licks they got in with their endless bickering and name calling. They thoroughly enjoyed their time together. Mattie said, "Well, there's the old fool against planting trees. You'd rather get sunburned, knot head!"

You poor excuse for an old cow, any trees you plant won't do you any good. You dead would be a comfort to me."

" Take some of your Southern Comfort to bed with ya. Maybe you'll die from it, you old bastard!"

"What's got into ya? I sure aint."

"Try it! I got a two by four waitin' for the occasion!"

"We was talkin' trees, not lumber, you old bat. Batty Mattie, ha."

Tomorrow it'll be my turn to walk two miles to holler over yer fence, Matt, the doormat. I'll wear my boots and stomp on you good, you come out to the street and down the block to the shade."

Arbor Day came. In the evening Batty Mattie could be seen digging in Matt's yard planting saplings for his grandkids to enjoy. He watched and said nothing.

STRICTLY WAX

The long winding staircase of the Sinclair Mansion was maple with a finish that placed it among the most exotic entries in the photo contest of Fashionable Interiors Magazine. The staircase had subtleties that erased shine and reflection.

Romance could be easily imagined.

The picture was glossy; but the staircase was light and understated. Banisters were ornate but simply presented. Its finish was strictly a wax, applied expertly, and showed the diligent care of one who was in love with being the caretaker.

The staircase whispered to the reader, "Look at me, look at me!"

CHEATING DOOMSDAY

The clock was ticking. The countdown to zero was approaching. A flip of a coin caused Armageddon to appear full strength, poised and ready for launch and containing enough fallout producing atomizer spray to poison all that lived on the planet: The cutie pies that lived in tree stumps and holes in the ground; the fast paced Gallagers that moved upon the earth and dominated all other creatures; the Chewing Chitzes that migrated upon the surface and devoured the dead---all were endangered.

War games organizers had simply chosen the planet at random for obliteration of life to further weapons study. All was a go and a three minute preliminary condition countdown was begun, checking all systems for errors. Suddenly an even more inviting planet came on screen. It was difficult to decide which would provide the greater results.

"Two out of three?"

"Sounds good."

Planet One was still targeted for the moment. Its designation was heads. The second toss came up tails as did the third toss.

New coordinates were entered into the systems and planet Two was doomed. It was doomed until an undetected error was loaded into the systems that caused a destructive explosion, dooming the killers and all life on the aggressor planet, Three.

BRING YOUR OWN ICECREAM

An Old Fashioned Ice Cream Social was advertised. Bring your own and add it to the mix. The Church of a Good God kicked off a new beginning in September with "something different".

Venders noticed a spike in sales on Saturday, September 11th. Remembrance prayers were on the agenda at the church. Droves of parishioners and friends drove to overflowing parking lots, church lots and nearby school lots. Side streets contained many vehicles.

Alice made her own ice cream in gallon lots and a pint for herself. She was housebound and her husband would go for both of them. He featured her on a widescreen display.

RECLINING PATSY

The recliner was Grandpa's. The recliner was Grandpa. Declining days were reclining days for the 79 year old former draftsman. His son-in-law had surprised him with a drafting board that fit over his knees and projected the surface of the board forward. He was ready to lay out his daughter's new home.

One day, while he dozed, his plans in front of him, grand children, Keith and Karen, came into the room and helped him with plans of their own. They practiced bunnies and chickens and stick figures and buses and cars. Then they carefully penned the word, "Suprize!" Ever after he put his plans aside when Keith and Karen visited. He provided them with planning paper.

COMPELLING REASON

Georgia O'Keeffe was a saint to the artist, Bridget Stellar. Admiration for the "Desert Rat", a name Bridget coined, was unbounded. Bridget's first showing was a success largely because she had endorsement from Georgia's heirs and her constant references to "The Desert Rat" as her inspiration. Of course, the showing was billed as a Stellar Exhibition, her husband's idea. A minor critic disagreed, citing a lack of good taste by a neophyte artist as a compelling reason to deny her acclaim which she had not earned, a compelling reason for him to be considered a minor critic.

CHARITABLE TAKING

Mary Koenig looked out of the window of the thrift store she managed. She watched Matt James make his way across the parking lot pushing his borrowed shopping cart containing discards he would donate at the receiving door. They would have to be picked through to be sure nothing valuable was missed.

Matt gave with a big heart and a love for helping others. What he gave was questionable at best. Most of it could only be considered worn out and of no value. No one would inform him his help was of little worth. It was obvious Matt wore discards that fit him. To him everything was "good stuff".

Mary made her way to the receiving door and thanked him for giving so much out of the little he had.

A GREAT DAY TO PROTEST

Flag waving along with shouts of acclamation for a cause coursed through a crowd of hundreds. A balmy late summer day was ideal for any outdoor activity. The organizers had taken the weather forecast into account in order to assure a large attendance and maximum media coverage.

A single pedestrian stopped to observe and realized he was opposed to the clamor and the cause. He began to pace the sidewalk with his own rancorous shouts.

Soon a policeman stopped the pedestrian's progress and issued him a citation for not having a permit to resemble a parade.

HA!

First, do no harm.
Why limit the concept to physicians?
Teach it in kindergarten and beyond, everywhere-HA!
No limits to passive goodness,
Second the first principle
Regarding the plowshare-HA!
Be reconciled one to the other. HA!
Seek redemption with purpose. HA!
Lion down with the lamb. HA!
Fish, not stones. Ha!
Get out of the misery business. HA!
Crooked to straight. HA!
Peaceful co-existence. HA! HA! HA!

SHARK'S TEETH

She stands at the gate
Bitchified,
And sells her pups in the form of loans.
She amasses fortunes from the masses,
Unmindful of their groans.
Shaded eyes and attractive smile
Win over whom wisdom would save.
And currency is a sought after prize,
Subduing whom,
Enriching a knave.

F.B.D.

(Flipping the bird democratically)
I hear angry democracites at play.
Shrill,
Throwing epithets and garish falsehoods—
Half truths—
While choosing sides.
The shell of maturity
Falls away
Revealing babble of insincerity,
Revealing schoolyard mentality,
Concealing context,
Appealing to self-serving egos,
Quarreling, with questionable intentions.
Handshakes have middle fingers extended.
Half-baked is used for enlightenment.
Arguments are slathered with spicy condiments.
Planes, trains, and automobiles
Are used for "appearance" sake.
Blowing smoke has the art of spin.
Anything goes to get a win.
Anything goes to get a win.

ANCHORED IN ILLUSION

Escher games defy the senses.
Optic senseless draws the eye
Toward sensory disproportion leading nowhere.
Eschering in a nonsense drawing aftershock applause
Appropriately silent night
Attached to sunlight under.
Non-Escher would be two of
Each would mirror its own reality.

FASCINATION WITH 'EM

The scary part is I won't let them go.
I finish poems and other pieces
Kept safely on a string only for myself.
They are ready to fling into the ocean of writing.
And, I can't help hoarding them.
My fascination with 'em is to blame.
Go for it! I tell myself.
But, will I?

THE STEW IS MARVELOUS:

POEMS FOR AN AFTERNOON

Carrots:
I thought I saw the leaves go down.
It was only in my imagination.
Summer into fall did stall
In its attempt to die a mini death.

Water:
I put the kettle on to boil some water.
I wanted tea; but coffee would do.
In the scheme of things it didn't really matter
To me, nor should it to you.

Potatoes:
I got seriously tangled in a love affair
With my wife of many years.
Off we go, all tangled together
In quiet living and a few tears.

Meat:
Meaty chunks of sitting together,
Commenting now and then,
Brings us to a point of no return
But never to a point of saying "when".

Gravy:
Today and all our yesterdays
Provide a lamp to see by
And takes us to all gracious living
As nights and days do fly.

PASTORAL OUTFITS

That Easter has sunshine.

Cool spring. Wear your old-timeys.
Gather in the park with umbrellas.
Promenade, young ladies, and your fellas.
Sunday in the park with Jennifer and George,
Sunday in the park with whoever is dandy,
Wander in the park licking ice cream, eating candy.

Long skirts, cut-a-ways, hats on parade—
All the couturiers have been over paid
For outfits pastoral, to be shown;
They are very varied. To each his own.

PASSIONATE INFLECTIONS

Serious emphasis rides around with laughter.
Comedy tries to outdo serious,
Making fun of the bark, the bite, the intoned expression.
Serious can take on subjects like "delirious",
Politics, the furious get-out-the-vote mentality,
The nobility of being God-like in appreciation of life, the
lilies of the field,
Saving lives through better medicine,
Making hairs black or white through chemistry.
The passionate inflections of comedy can do the same.

CAUSTIC BIBLE READER

So, God is a trickster, turning conventional thought up-side-down! Who would have thought it was necessary! There He goes again, calling the tongue-tied Moses to speak for Him. There He goes again, testing Abraham, whose son looks like a delicious sacrifice.

The gentle Giant called kings and they responded. Indolence raised its ugly head, to be chastised. "Doest thy meager understanding fail to connect with the magnitudious meaning of the grand idea?"!

There's that sacrifice again by one who rejects sacrifice. Called the Christ, The son of God, the Lamb, the way, the life, there was nothing for it but that the Son of God should be killed. So, God did need sacrifice! Who would have thought it was necessary.

CHECKS AND BALANCES

A man walks into a haberdashery. He says, "I need to try on some new outfits. What do you have?" The clerk says, "We have suits with matching ties. We have slacks and jackets for mix and match. What do you prefer?" The man thinks for a minute, matching his capacity, and says, "I've always wanted to see how I'd look in checks." The clerk says, "Walk this way." The man imitates the clerk's waddle to the mix-and-match. The man picks out red checks in a jacket and yellow checks in slacks. He returns them to the rack after trying them on. After seeing himself in a mirror, he selects solids and considers the checkered passed.

ABSURD NOTIONS

A monarch wanted his cities to be spick and span, devoid
of dirt and trash and anything disagreeable. So, the
people went about cleaning and made all the Bastard's
cities gleam.

Teach a blind man to use all of his senses. Teach a
senseless man to close his blinds. Peek-a-boo!

Sprits of air freshener under the arms and all over
nudity—Use shoe polish to color the hair. Use your
camera widely to take a self portrait.

Legend has it Jesus had to die.

CONCERTINA CONCERTO, TINA

Squeeze boxes were the primary instruments in
playing music for royalty in Letharioburg in the small
independent country of Liebedu. A concert was held
every year on May 1st in honor of the reigning king,
Herman. In the year 1619.Maria and her friend of twenty
one years had invitations acquired by her aunt, the Royal
Duchess, Hermina. The event was to be her new friend's
first. Both were excited. Maria said, "Wait until you hear
the Concertina Concerto, Tina!

ASSURED DEVOTIONS

The brick church had a prayer room off the sanctuary where anyone could go for study and devotions. A sign over the door called for silence. A feel of a small library prevailed. A closed door provided a soundproof barrier to the outside. A few parishioners even preferred using the room to services, and confined their time to personal worship.

Cramped for space, the new pastor began to use the room as a place to write sermons. Then he began to entertain visitors who called on him.

Unknown to him, others who would use the room came and went, not wanting to intrude. The pastoral relations committee was notified of their concerns. The committee chairperson said," No more" to the pastor who gave assurance the room would henceforth be deemed for devotions only.

The pastor moved his sessions with visitors to the sanctuary where they went largely uninterrupted. Space was not a problem, and devotions were assured.

JACK, WON AND LOST

Jack Doulowkalowskalowski watched the wheel turn round and round as he stood in silent wonder in the doorway of the saloon his father frequently attended. He knew he would have to turn a wheel like that someday; and in his dreams he saw himself a very lucky fellow, winning millions of the little round pieces his father every night exchanged for money. He was a chip off the old block, so to speak; but his ambitions certainly exceeded the bounds of sobriety to an even greater extent than his father's thirst for whiskey.

His father was all that he had in the way of family; and when they parted company that night, he was all alone in the world. If his father had had no thirst to be exceeded, they would still be together. But, with a half dozen shots under his belt, Mr. D. was in no mood to explain in a patient way to his son the impropriety of a boy of fourteen subjecting himself to the evil influences of the place Mr. D. often referred to as a three ring circus. Jack saw his father approach him in a menacing manner, reaching with his hand to steady himself as he came along between the tables, touching nothing, but seeming to find something in the nothing to keep him from falling. He laid hands on the boy and threw him forcefully into the street, then turned and staggered back to continue his performance at the wheel of chance. He won more money that night than ever before; but he lost what he prized above all else, the hero worship of his son. He never saw his son again and died in a few years of a broken ego.

HOW GROSS IS THE FOUNTAIN

Showers of blessing that fall on the blessed and the
unblessed
Fountains away what has been sullied as God is second
guessed
And no good purpose is served by the blowing up of
children

God goes away on explosion day from monsters' excuses,
Not a party to the placing of His little ones in harm's way
The fountain, not working, lies dormant this judgment
day

Weeds grow in the rotting fountain base years after the
dying
Under forces that find purpose in the tears of the crying
For, Evil takes death for granted in sludging toward
perfection

Oh, for pity's sake! They're expendable in light of our
need!
They don't feel a thing; their little bodies don't really
bleed!
As propaganda from leaders sullies the fountain with
poison

How gross is the fountain devoid of the showers of
blessing
In ugliness of stagnation, infestation fear, second
guessing,
Snuffing the breath from minor intrusions on terror
reprisal

Showers of blessing that fall on the blessed and
unblessed
Fountain away what has been sullied as God is second
guessed
And no good purpose is served by the blowing up of
children

FORBIDDEN FRUIT

God is kept away from fruit a man has declared
forbidden,
The millstone growing heavier with the passing years,
Until he is overcome by weariness and his death occurs.
Then the sins of the fathers accumulate on youthful
shoulders
Full circle; forbidden fruit is forever unrelated to God.

�֍ �֍ ✖

REFLECTIONS

A LITTLE PINE

A little pine will take its time
To reveal the "large" inside.
Some years will come and go
Without its revealing much,
As multiplying needles grow.
A little pine is insignificant to know.
But, love takes over just the same
And lasts a lifetime in light or gloom of night,
All picture perfect in pure delight
For a pine tree by a tomb.

NOW, LET US BE BRAVE

The teacher is whoever or whatever transfers knowledge.
It comes in the stricken wreck of tragic occurrences,
Including mind places, hiding repetitive excursions.
Bells bring in happiness as time circumvents wrecks;
And there is much to create out of whatever vexes.

Now, let us be brave and piece together lives
And rejoice.
Forgiveness and love come out of wrecks of life.
And joy comes out of newness of life.

I UNDERSTAND PRECIOUS

Out of the whirlwind that is life and breath and strife
and death,
Out of casualty count in spite of what has always been
feared,
Out of reports of snuffing out lives as if they didn't
matter,
Out of a child's laughter and sense of what constitutes
delight,
Out of the "Look up and live" that points to a concerned
God,
Out of stories of gloom and what constitutes too much of
everything,
Out of rebellion over nothing that could count as being
significant,
Out of reports of beginnings by those who would
challenge,
I gain an understanding of "Precious".

POOLSIDE CHAT

Two bathers sat poolside in conversation.
They could be twins from what anyone could tell,
Though one had distorted features now and then.
Something there was in each of celebration
That neither of them could quite quell.
And they were synchronized, if they chose to turn on a dime.

No words were exchanged out loud.
They were sure not to draw a crowd,
They were sure neither of them had committed a crime.
Though, sitting at a poolside might be considered so.
They were, upon reflection, of the same mind
About such things as the daily grind for dough.

Peace like a river entered suddenly and with overwhelming force.
There was no time for pondering reasons for remorse
For being scarred after being shot and reflection bared the truth.
"All brillig were the slithy toves." They had faced the Jabberwok.
Now they sat in peacefulness to talk and talk and talk.

FINALLY PRETTY

She stood tall at a large window and looked out upon her
city.
Euphoria now lacked its initial charm as calmness looked
back at Hell.
Her glow from being successful lost out to the cost along
the way—to the top!
Pinnacle was still an upward glance,
Though she felt comfortable wearing pants;
And there was still a chance for higher.
"Work harder, girl," she intermixed with chagrin over the
"never-to-be-retrieved".
There was only "up" to look forward to, she believed.
"Mary, you've got to put your stamp on the world.
"Mary, don't forget to keep your hair curled.
"Mary, you can do better than that!
"Mary, you had best marry for convenience and money.
"Mary, don't be contrary and experiment with carefree.
"Mary, don't be merry; stick to the wheel of fortune."
And she did.
Forty-two and proud and merciless in her way with
others,
Mary had merit symbols up the wazoo in cars and clothes
and loveless life.

Something broke. She began to choke, wishing her whole
damn life she could revoke!
There was nothing of happy she could go back to for
comfort.
(Her father, of consequence, was so enamored of her top
of the ladder syndrome.

He was a gnome of the world of finance who controlled a
lot of gold.
Ebenezer was a squeezer for his own gain and sharked
his way into prominence.
His was entirely a world of dominance.
His was the way of a weasel.)

"Mother"! And no comforting echo replied.

Mary crumbled and it was all over.
She left the suite and slammed the door, her resignation
left behind.
She left, "cold turkey," the nitty-gritty grind.
She clicked her heels and sang, "I feel pretty. A new life
I will find."

THE ELEPHANT PRETENDS

An elephant named Suzy
Felt a bit woozy and lay on her side one day.
Elephant tricks were part of the mix
As on her side she did lay.
"I'll make a dust angel," she thought.
It was a fine one she wrought
To take flight on let's-pretend wings.
When an elephant tries, an elephant flies
And does other lets-pretend things.

A SINGULAR SAILBOAT

On a lake behind a dam
A singular sailboat is toy-like
From where I am.

On a lake of placid stillness
A sailboat, sail of white, is
Perfection I will confess.

On a lake for recreation
The silent portrait of a sailboat
Betrays its celebration.

On a lake of listlessness comes praise
Of what is serenely grand,
Belying effort of every word or phrase.

On a lake, where no noises exist,
Pacifying the Artist's eye for fun
Brings forth a sailboat gently kissed
By sun.

SIGNATURE HATS

Taught to fish at an early age, Emerson Bradbury waded offshore and cast a whistling line to mid stream, again and again. He had a still and very respectful audience who was ten and named Will. Emerson called him Will·o·the Wisp. Yet, when they went fishin', Will was attentive and steadfast in his desire to be a great fisherman, too.

Emerson's catches were legendary, and, made more magnificent with each telling. One day, according to Blaze Gilbert, his casting was whip out, whip back forty·two times with forty two fish, each of which just fell off the line. Mason Goodman remembered Emerson's thirty inch trout that would have made Ripley's if they had taken a picture.

Those who had Made Emerson a legend, including Emerson, met over drinks on Saturday nights. They all wore their signature "Liar's Club" hats and held a roast for their honored guest.

Will, of course, was excluded. However, he had his own, unique, "Gone Fishin'" signature hat. It was just as good as Emerson's fishin' hat, tied flies and all.

THE OLD HAT

It stood vertical on a peg in an empty home
Unblocked, odd shaped, water spattered crown that had
dried,
An abandoned hat, lonely as a cloud,
Never lately had been lifted down and tried.

Now, a man of means and culture viewed the interior of
the house
While contemplating fixing up the place to sell it at a
profit.
His face reflected in window light espied the old
abandoned hat.
He took it down. His boyish grin came from deep within,
And reversed, as he shed a tear over what might have
been.
The hat fit snugly; but, in the looking glass he saw his
father.
Looking back at him was the image of one who had died.

PRIME, AIRY COLORS

Primo! Primo! Primo! Primo were the colors seemingly in flight that adorned the creations of Wally McIntire. Her spring collection made the whew reverberate across the audience; and the applause, in unison, brought a glow to her cheeks. Basically primary colors in maddeningly diverse shades and hues prevailed.

Success was hers in only her third outing. Delicate red scarf accented an off white bloused shirt jacket worn outside a hunter green solid color skirt with pleats stole the show. The knockoffs with her name would pay for Paris in the fall.

Fully awake, her job as a seamstress and pin lady demanded her attention for another day of reality, though she could still hear the applause.

COURSE CORRECTION

Red Chief be damned! Mean wittle kid, pooh!

Jamie Just-enough-to-drive-her-parents-crazy Smith put those boys to shame. She was not just a daredevil. She was constantly pushing a curl aside as acts of abomination were performed in perpetual motion. She picked on little kids. She flung boogers against the bathroom wall and laughed at her mother's shriek. She was even spanked once to no avail.

Jamie was so smart she gave teachers fits. She filled a lot of vacant class time with mischief. It was a personal badge of honor when she failed her conduct grade. Counselors gave up on her. Getting expelled only put her parents in more peril. She was headed for a life of drugs and violence everyone was convinced.

She never walked when she could skip or run. Mrs. Mower came toward her on a sunny day. Mrs. Mower, in her wheel chair, made no move to avoid the child. Moving aside, Jamie stopped and reached to tip the chair.

"Try it!" A course cackle said loudly. A cane came out from under a lap cover. "Stay put! Sit down! Now listen!" Mrs. Mower's voice changed. It was smoother, calming.

Jamie sat, frustrated and confused. There was no fear to dominate.

The voice told of a brat many years ago who endangered others and herself and who wound up in a wheel chair and alone.

Strangely warmed, Jamie became a companion to a voice of compassion. The two of them were inseparable until Mrs. Mower died. Jamie went on to become a Mrs. Mower not alone.

CHEERUP, THE OLD LADY

The infant wailed, and so often, her parents gave her the unusual name of Cheerup.

Now, Cheerup grew in wisdom and stature; but her maturity found her forever in one situation after another that stressed her to the point of tears. She was never satisfied until she had rattled one cage or another. She worked tirelessly to attain perfection in all she took on. And, it was overwhelming, yet addictive. She ran herself ragged even into old age.

In the home for the aged she complained about everything and cried, sometimes out loud. Jamie Smith, cane in hand, said to an attendant, Come on. Let's cheer up the old lady.

WOK CHALK TALK

Chef Harry Wong began his cooking classes by saying he could talk the wok. At the chalk board he began with a simple mix of meat, vegetables and complements, along with his own special sauce. At the end of the lesson everyone would know the secret of his sauce. That meant they never failed to be attentive. It was special in everyone's mind. Its secret was that it was always passed along.

FIRM HANDLING

Gracie Up Along Side and Down was a curious race horse whose gentility made her strut. Hers was the curse of such breeding as was commensurate with her attitude. She forbade anyone to touch her until it was time for her to be presented, paraded and pampered by applause···anyone, that is, except her groom, the golden boy of the stables, Michael McGowan.

Michael was flinty-eyed. His curt gestures, along with assurances couched in staccato speech, seemed to quiet the filly and assuage her rebellion. It was a case of firm handling, acquiescence, and the taming of a shrew.

IN THE SIDE POCKET

Stoked on beer and free peanuts, Al Pace spends his days at "The President". His local billiards parlor has been good to him in the five years he has lived in Goodman. His trick shots, practiced all day, in the evening bring in tips that fill a sizeable mug with as much as a hundred and fifty dollars. Scores of people are fascinated and mesmerized by impossible shots he has invented and that he makes look easy.

Al Pace likes to pace himself and will break before he breaks the rack to meet a challenge. He will sit and jaw with someone, relax, get away from the concentration and clear his mind as a connoisseur clears his pallet. Then he will display such skill with a cue as will beat the pants off the challenger. Some challenge just to get him going.

Al's "loser shot" gives him the most pleasure. He raffles off a shot. He lines three balls evenly spaced from one side of the table to the other. He bets the corner pocket to his right. The cue ball must pass between balls, come back and kiss the nine ball into the named corner pocket. Everyone knows what is coming. The cue ball hits the outer edge ball that stalls with reverse spin and falls into the side pocket. Not a particularly difficult shot. But, the raffle number is selected and read and someone goes home a winner.

TENOR, ELEVEN, WAITING TO ASSAIL

He was not yet a tenor—more like a soprano. Range, tone, breathing were all there. He was called, affectionately, Pea Brain because his intelligence and his talent were recognized from an early age as a force that needed to be controlled if he were to have a satisfying life in the world of music.

Mario Rellano did numbers in his head that danced into solutions. Sugar plums were mere background to enhance images. He was spoken of in hushed tones of admiration as a prodigy. Far from savant, Mario had glass shattering quality to his high C and purity of sustained tone that gave waves of chills to audiences.

Voice change could have turned him away from music had he been given a lesser lot in life than to be the son of determined parents. They would not focus their attention toward anything else. He would not strain his voice. Instead, he could study piano for a year or two then rehearse as Tenor extraordinaire.

Too much too soon caused him to want freedom to search for his own identity apart from his gifted talents. All he could have been went begging into his fortieth year. He still lived at home with severely chastened parents who blamed themselves for being too strict.

The parents died that year within weeks of each other. Suddenly Mario took on a persona out of guilt that caused him to become a strict disciplinarian. Too late. What could have been shaped and molded into a grand career could not be recovered and left him forever waiting to assail tremendous heights of success.

PASTA LA VISTA, BABY

Goodbye to whatever is strained and pasted.
Goodbye to the baby food jar.
Goodbye to the itty bitty spoon, the milk bottle, the
toothless grin.
Hello..........spaghetti, pasgetti, whatever is pasta,
potato, porridge.
Yummy is the pasta, Baby.

PANDA THINK

The old grey panda has a vacant stare.
The panda is like a teddy bear in slow motion.
It's hard to tell if the stare is hiding a notion
That man is weird, indeed—
Look and point and mill around, and move—
Distinctly garbed.
They have their "other side" on which to walk and ride,
Uncontrolled and free.
I don't know why they don't just sit and chew a shoot,
like me.

AW! TOE INFECTION SUGGESTION

If your toe offends you, cut it off.
Now, there is a suggestion that is Biblical.
It's not too late to deal with infection
That is, in a sense, un-Biblical!
Talk to it in chastising tones.
Perhaps it will yield to correction.
Give it wide berth in danger zones
To keep it safe from ow-full obstructions.
Test it gingerly in a few days
To see if clearing up will amaze
Even your particularly surly phase.
Perhaps your gate will improve to normal
When the owie is no longer noticeable.
Perhaps a joke will come to mind
And a smile will make you less formal.
If your toe now gets no sympathy,
Perhaps you can develop a cough.

AUNT TILLIE'S MOUNTAIN

She knew her Tin Lizzy inside and out. She could fix it. She could start it when it balked. Warm or cold, sunny days found Tillie Crawford exploring the back roads of her mountain, something puny at 6200 feet and unnamed. Yet, everyone expected her at Old Mill for a sit down lunch at the Speaker Café. She was Aunt Tillie to everyone on her mountain.

When she discovered a home in a place she had never been, she only had to knock and say, "I'm Aunt Tillie." That was only the password she needed, talking as long as her hosts could allow. She introduced them to her history of the Old Timers who came down from the mountain only at their turn to take up permanent residence in Belmont Cemetery.

KANG

Fabulous Freddie worked with precision to become the best football player he could be. His regimen that he prescribed for himself was as dedicated as that of a tri-athlete, a cyclist or a marathon runner. He was a Rocky with a purpose, foregoing much that would have made him a well rounded individual. In high school and college he was tutored to a grade of C; and he slid by. During classes he focused on dynamic tension exercises. He was oak hard and weight lifter muscled.

Freddy Chance gave himself every chance to go pro and impress with his prowess. He still felt he needed a shtick that would stick and give him a nickname that would be touted by announcers and give him recognition. He could outrun most D B'S and early on caught admiring looks.

It was Freddie's habit after catching the ball to race ahead with time to stop, put both feet together and hop across the goal line. The maneuver garnered the nickname "Roo" for kangaroo.

"That's not boo," the announcer would say. "They're saying Roo for Freddy Chance, the kangaroo." One sarcastic fan of an opponent asked, "Does he carry the ball in his pouch?"

EVERYWHERE TITULAR

The title of titular head of state
Reflected puppet strings for a surrogate.
The titular title of an underling
Was grandiose but didn't mean a thing
As long as the underling was subservient
And understood what it really meant
To have the title but have no sting.

"Titular! Titular! Titular!" "Sir?"

Everywhere the nothings have no say
And regularly posture for their pay,
Exiting from the modern scene
When inconvenient their role does mean.
And they move up from being titular
To sporting a titular of their own—
Who is perfectly willing to assume the throne.

ACTUAL INCIDENT

It actually happened that a large man took "All you can eat" to extremes at his favorite Deli over a period of seven years. It actually happened that the large man heaped his plate three times, downed three colas and three desserts. It actually happened that the large man was rushed to the hospital after foraging one day and was diagnosed as having an acute gas attack. It actually happened that he was placed on a diet and antacids and that he lost a hundred and twenty pounds and had to replace his wardrobe three times and still wore loose-fitting clothes. He ate veggies, salads, and egg whites and drank healthy shakes. It actually happened that he quit smoking and alcohol and everything unhealthy. His personal hygiene was elevated to the point of his grooming himself for "show dog" of the year. It actually happened that he found a girl to marry and on their wedding night he collapsed and died. She had fixed him a seven course meal and a leafy salad for herself. "Bon Voyage," She said cheerfully and left the house to cash his insurance policy.

INHARMONIOUS CACOPHONY

Ahhh, Kazoo and a "bless you"
Puts the instrument in its place.
Cacophonous Kazooing is monotonous
When little instrumentalists learn to play.
With a zoo-zoo here and a zoo-zoo there
Here a zoo, there a zoo
Zoo here, zoo there, zoo-zoo everywhere.
Hoo-hoo, hoo-hoo, hoo-hoo, hoo.

ODD NOVEMBER

It began with a leftover dandelion,
Puffy heads un-blown.
Frozen, they seemed to be, in time.
The cause was unknown.
Even snow caused a sense of mime
Of something that had actually grown
White, insubstantial, yet permanent.
It was alone, marvelous to behold,
And it seemed to be a mystery to unfold
Before its eventual clearance
Of any resemblance to present appearance.

Odd November gave in to something charming
As its introduction to something disarming.
Cold mixed with warm in November days
That mixed bright colors with blue and grays.

�֍ �֍ ✖

MISCELLANEOUS CHATTER

MESSING WITH THE BARD

Avon calling! Where is our Bard?
A gentle man with a bent for pleasing,
For leaving a genius' calling card,
For tucking some humor and some teasing
Into what would otherwise be ugly.

Avon calling! You've made a mess;
And nothing can assuage one's pure loathing
Of shortened scenes and modern dress
And other sorts of different clothing.
Don't make a change. Bring back beauty.

Poor Richard is all maniac;
And Duncan is a frosted donut.
Both are authored by a brainiac.
George is proof that kings go nuts.
Just keep them all Elizabethan.

Do your messing with lesser playwrights
Who have nothing in the way of stature,
Who should go outside and fly kites
Instead of basking in William's rapture.
Take unadulterated as a text to follow.

MAGNIFICENT ATTRACTIONS

Bits and pieces of imported cheese
Surround the wheels and wedges
Like satellites, foiled and sealed.
Attractive in their wrappers, edges
Taunting, as colors are revealed.

Bright labels call out to shoppers,
"Delight in our taste today.
Our recipe is right for weight loss,
So Doctors so and so and so and so say.
Have a cookie without calories to floss."

Look at the greens of pickles, yellows,
Eye-level displays, including gherkins,
Evoking eye-watering emotions,
Speaking of relish dishes your kin
Folk will savor like magic potions.

Veggie colors in tantalizing splendor
Toss salads into those brightening eyes
That wander amid a produce section
Of A and P or other grocery vendors
Whose mix is of earth grown selection.

There are yellows, reds, greens···
From cantaloupe to varied beans,
From various peppers to all onions,
To show what fresh to lush means,
When measured by the pound from tons.

WBD CLUTCHING AT TREASURE

Book title "The White Boned Demon":
Madam Mao put on trial.
Repent or die! In two years.
cha-ching! Jiang Quing!
Grow toward subtle greatness
In imitation of an awkward doll.
Ibsening, she flung herself toward independence.

A star was born obscurely,
A girl child rebelled against her duty.
Theater trained her for her station
And placed her next to violation
In a political arena.

Shut up. Told to shut up, shut up, shut up.
Sew the dolls, sew the dolls, sew the dolls.

DEEP THROATED YARN SPINNERS

They go on line then get away and yak.
They consider themselves good at tacking, turning and
yapping about their skills.
School's out for them as they play hooky, swimming,
splashing in rainbow arcs,
Testing fishermen's wills.

They are deep throat, cut throat, line snappers.
They brag in their fish stories as they tell how they got
away.
They tell how in their deep pools they are nappers;
Until something delicious has wormed its grey way down;
Or a feathered something has come from town.

Cat lumbers with wicked splash then heavily makes a
dash, gets free, regurgitates metal and makes his point
when the wound heals.
Tuna is taught to the tune of a hickory stick and learns
the price of "hauled in and peeled".
Mostly, its fate is sealed.
Trout will have it out with the fly guy.
Herring will realize a net worth of freedom if it slips the
surly bonds of string in mirth—and lives.

A carp is carping;
A trout is pouting;
A blow hole is spouting;
Flyers are winging;
Minnows are springing;
Eels are stinging;
Cockles are shelling;
Shell fish are selling;

Their counterparts ride the surface and patiently wait—
And use their hands to communicate what got away.

SHUFFLING COLES

Porter and Nat King and Old King and Natalie, in full
swing,
And Nat King and Natalie in full throated sing of Cole
Porter.
Mix some Cole at the piano before a low fire.
Fire a log or two.
Wander off to fulfill a heart's desire.
Dream fiddlers play.
Interpretation can bring on sleep in the afterglow.

I LIKE PERSPECTIVE

Deepening, enlarging, softening, diminishing
Depiction takes the eye to where
The sight has focus and then is blurred;
And reproduction takes one to satisfaction
When something magic has occurred.

I like to gaze at masterpieces,
Un-surreal, and, large and smaller teases,
Tasking me to make comparison
To how things really do appear,
When projections exhibit far and near.

DRINK

He built himself a small cocoon
And never fluttered wings
Until he learned to crawl.
He never learned the butterfly's things
Until he hit a strong wall,
Taking all he had to ruin.
Quick and slow flight, with flow to alight,
Took him to a nectar for survival
That welcomed profusely his arrival.

OF DUCKS AND SUCH

I saw a duck in low flight
Across a pedestrian walkway
Unto splashdown beside a fountain spray.
So much is life of value
When such is made of flight.

I looked upon a single Iris flag of orange
And wondered how many flag days are in an Iris.
There had to be at least the one today
That added greatly to my bliss.

I observed a cat in pause.
It licked a paw and washed.
The momentous is subordinate clause, in essence,
To a cat's look of independence.

I put imagination in a mouse's flash
While scurry meant a lot to a little furry.
I tried to see it dart to safety;
But my mind was in a hurry.

I totaled up my experiences
In spite of all the gates and fences
That surrounded territories
 Circumscribing my living stories.

The sum of all that came to me
Overcame my summing sense.
I hope that I'm around to see it all
When, next, rejuvenating acts commence.

CAT'S ASLEEP

Nose tucked under tail tip,
Silent, slow, rhythmic breathing,
Unconscious, eyes closed, cat's slip
Away to good "perchance to dream"
Wanderings among the unaware
Give pause amid curled up paws
And silence.

CAT'S UP

When the cat gets up
And I expand my activity
To fulfill her wishes,
It is then I think
She should get up high
And help me with the dishes.

Cat wants out and wants in.
Cat wants a bit of chicken.
Cat will sit in a doorway
To give herself a lickin'.
When cat gets up, I pat her butt
And think she belongs in Norway.

When cat gets up from an all day sleep
Then lies upon the table,
My finger scratchin' she will enable
With words that are subject to a bleep.

HALLOWEEN CAT

She of the calico persuasion in tiny fur ball status lay upon the orange and black couch cushion almost invisible.

Weaned and plopped down in an alien world, she slept.

Diligent care made sure she was not sat upon—that upon waking she could drink, dine, litter and sleep again.

Long hair stood out this way and that and made a fuzzy cuteness. White and black paws, whiteness in the face, gave delighted pause to a casual observer.

Kitten status faded and blurred into floor-to-high perch in a single bound, into faster than a speeding bullet around the house in chase of her reflection or another feline outside a window, in quick time, thumpity-thump-thump across the floor.

Eighteen Halloweens she decorated where she slept or perched or strode. Orange and black of a Halloween cat gave a unique touch to the children's day. Then, silently dreaming and very still, she slipped away.

ELDER'S TURN

This elderly cat turns slowly.
It changes sides in one minute flat.
It has ascended to its sitting height,
It has scratched and nibbled,
And it has stared, in still-life mode.
It has descended, to lie still in sleep.

SILENT CONVERSATION

A look, a smile, a comfort feeling
For two in close proximity;
A glance, a certain goofy stance,
Portend mockily to offend;
A touch, a kiss, a U-turn in a narrow miss,
Provide the envelope for a message to send.

A raised brow in query,
A promise in a smile,
A point to a yellow daffodil,
To a bird upon a windowsill,
A hand squeeze in acknowledgement
Of a sparrow or a whippoorwill:
All suggest communication.

UNCLE SAM HAS SOME PARKS

Teddy R., John Muir, names
talking of wilderness for all time,
Set-asides known for grandeur,
Places of drive-through—
Places of awe-inspiring—
Places of square miles by the millions--
Territories are untouchables.

Safely observe. Do not stray.
Take in majestic, ocean, forest, snowcaps, canyons.
Take in lakes and mirrored images, wild life.

Forestry Service, management, rules,
Setting fires by blaspheming fools,
 Daring trekking and getting lost
Unmindful of the cost
Tourists in ant-like progressions
Fulfilling their "go there" obsessions.

ACADIA

Stone, moss, grey-blue sea,
Desert Island, desert,
People—what they have wrought,
Thunderous blow hole from cavernous hole,
Little train around a short track,
Winding road,
Much like a giant fist
Protecting Frenchman Bay.

The sea slams and granite resists.
Stone brightens with green and red.
White pine, forest, wharf, dinghies,
And "let's fish" flavors sixty thousand acres.

SMOKIES

Outside Gatlinburg is a climb to iridescent beauty and a
waterfall.
Up, and into grays and reds and greens and all manner
of rain producing vegetation.
Old reduced mountains harbor old and massive trees and
thunderous creeks to whet the appetite to fish and whet
the appetite for fish.
Joyce Kilmer is remembered.
Cherokee are reservation-ed.
Clingman is domed.
Baldo are mystifying.
Shared by states, the Smoky Mountain Park transcends
borders, and lure.
No one resented the park.
F.D.R. presented the park.
And, eight hundred miles of trails went every which way
through half a million acres.

EVERGLADES

Everglades of marsh meadow, siphoned, park protected,
give untamed life and being a chance.
They will be controlled and allowed to exist.
Pines and willows and hammocks and seas of grasses and
fish, herons, too.
Gators are lurkers and waiters.
Where the sea forgot to end, great cities gave it
boundaries;
Then did killing of miles of wetland end.

BIG BEND

Landscaping in anticipation of Rio Grande gorging
Sits amidst "Rainbows waiting for rain".
God's landfill,
Useless for all but the hardy who adobe and farm out of
flooding.
The park has roads; the park's rock is carved so ugly it
has strange beauty.
The park sits on a bend in Texas and waits⋯
Patiently it waits.
Vultures patiently circle. Rabbits hurriedly run.
Humanity in small numbers gets an eyeful and moves on.
It could have remained unused except it is there—
A giant contradiction.
It straddles a river for hundreds of miles.

GRAND CANYON

Go West, restless waters—
Stop. Divide, conquer rocks that give way over eons and
paint in depth gorgeous gorges.
Arizona Grande carved by a busy Colorado River
Deified country unused to superlatives until language
caught up to emotion.
Mules go down.
Mules come up.
Riders get to the bottom of things, peering into the
depths, exclaiming
"Oh! my God!"

YELLOWSTONE

Up from the ground comes bubbling broiling mud.
Geysers rise one hundred, three hundred feet.
They spray and shower their surroundings.
By the clock, they are always on time.
Old Faithful helps itself to fame.

Flowers in a granny land, older than all the other parks,
Surface in all the other surroundings.
Yellowstone River runs through it.
Yellowstone Park quietly sits idly with its bison, big
horns, bounty in wildlife.
It saws off the northwest corner of Wyoming.

Teddy R., John Muir, names
Talking of wilderness for all time,
Set-asides known for grandeur,
Places of drive-through—
Places of awe-inspiring—
Places of square miles by the millions--
Territories as untouchables
Safely observe. Do not stray.
Take in majestic, ocean, forest, snowcaps, canyons.
Take in lakes and mirrored images, wild life.
Forestry Service, management, rules,
Setting fires by blaspheming fools,
 Daring trekking and getting lost
Unmindful of the cost.
Tourists in ant-like progressions
Fulfilling their "go there" obsessions.

YOSEMITE

"An eagle souring above a sheer cliff, where I suppose its nest is, makes another striking show of life, and helps to bring to mind the other people of the so-called solitude—deer in the forest caring for their young; the strong, well-clad, well fed bears; the lively throng of squirrels the blessed birds, great and small, stirring and sweetening the groves...all these come to mind...but most impressive of all is the vast glowing countenance of the wilderness in awful, infinite repose."   John Muir 1869

"No temple made with hands can compare with Yosemite. Every rock in its walls seems to glow with life."

John Muir   1869

Awesome valley, shaped over 200,000,000 years.
Majestic are the cliffs in high rise;
North Dome, Half dome, El Capitan!
Sequoia giants planted firmly as towering reminders of long ago.
Glacier Point looks on a view of unstable earth.
Weather and eruption have created something sublime.
Amazing distortions have created beauty.
A great Yosemite Falls and punctuates massive drops.
Things could change over 200,000,000 years.

OLYMPIC

Mountains have their own Olympics.
Snowcapped, they vie for purple majesty in Olympic
National Park;
Mount Olympus has surmounted all of its competition.
John Meares preceded Zebulon Pike in naming a
champion.

Peninsular, 1400 square miles include mountains pushed
up from the sea.
Rainforests, forests, forests, forests, bordering
reservation;
Misty strangeness pervades everything.
Wildlife migration to lush high country occurs in
summer.
Retreat to the valleys in winter completes a cycle.
And, Serenity, thy name is Olympic.

DENALI

Mount. McKinley, king of the range,
Denali to the natives, towers over Wonder Lake.
Dall sheep are everywhere.
Ptarmigans fly everywhere.
Tundra leads to mountains.
Wolves come and go.
Denali stands in grandeur.
Three times the size of Yellowstone,
The park is captured for all time.
Take a train for a twenty hour ride.

HAWII, HAWAII VOLCANO

Rockin' volcano, blow your top.
Then blacken where lava flows to the sea.
"Hawaii?"
"Fine, Hawaii?"
Kilauea is a lulu. Its crater forms a park.
Redden the sky then blacken the earth
And silently rumble for all you're worth.
Volcano, volcano, make the landscape dark,
Two thousand miles from somewhere park.
Aren't you voluminous and stark!

ATTRIBUTION

UNCLE SAM HAS SOME PARKS SOURCE:
NATIONAL PARKS—READER'S DIGEST—
EXPLORE AMERICA

�✕✕

THE CARRADINE BRAND

A LIFE IN A SERIES OF VIGNETTES

Forward

The order of the episodes is inconsequential, since they are brought forward by Hetty Carradine and, in the last episode, by Elizabeth Martin. The order is a shuffled deck and placing them in order would be tedious and would do injustice to the heroine whose reflections give rise to the story.

A JIG OF ROMANCE

Long dark tresses surrounded an oval face. The nose was too large. Somberly she sat on a stump at the edge of the field and pondered the beyond. Having picked up a clod of dirt, she crumbled it and let the siftings fall. She crumbled another and another.

Indians in the Black Hills still roamed in bands and sometimes fought the Government. But that was a long way from Minor County. The Minnesota border was ten miles to the East. That was a good measure of safety.

Hetty McKennna was sixteen and alone. Mother and Dad were too old. Johnny and Ira were too young—babies. Her hero hadn't come yet. She sat patiently.

Out of the heat shimmer a figure appeared, more and more distinctly. Alfred, after what seemed an hour, spoke.

"Hetty, I leave tonight for the front. Pray that we shall meet again. I love you and would forgo the call to war if you would but speak the word."

"Love you not honor more?"

"Please don't say the word."

"Ha, ha, Alfred, please be romantic or I'll have to ask you to leave."

"Oh, yes. Well if I must. Darling, let's dream of the day when we'll marry. I'll come with a brace of snow white horses and a carriage. I love you."

"I love you." Hetty lingered over the phrase. Would she ever say it aloud to a real man?

Enough f'daddle. This wasn't getting Bessy home. She picked up her switch. The family cow cooperated somewhat slowly but with little urging.

Granger McKenna had a terse, no nonsense way of expressing himself. Yet he was gentle rather than overbearing. His daughter had taken lately to dallying. He sympathized; but it did not square with his need to have things in their place and done on time. Waste not want not applied to time as well as to money, food or whatever.

"Hetty, girl, don't dally. Get Bessy in her stall.
You've still to milk her. Yer ma's waitin' for help with
supper. Day dreamin' best be left for the night." His
logic always went unquestioned. His truths were often
couched in contradiction; and Hetty wasn't sure it wasn't
by design. He seemed bent on making a point
remembered.

Hetty en-stalled Bessy with a swat. Milking did
not absorb her attention, which wandered toward the
gaze of Alfred. He stood there, tall, blond—'muggededly-
uggedly", she thought. That didn't fit. She was
momentarily bewildered. For, Alfred was really fair and
handsome, with a rather slight build. This one's speech
was course and strangely rough.

"Hi, I'm Will Carradine. Your Pa hired me to cut
fire wood." The ax dandled loosely from his massive
hand.

Fiddlesticks! He had no right to invade her
privacy with small talk. This giant lacked a great deal to
be worthy of her. She mentally measured herself beside
him. An estimate of five foot four inches against six foot
six inches, broad shoulders and bulging muscles
made her laugh.

"Perhaps you should do what you were hired to do.
I don't have time to converse with you."
"You're Hetty. Your Pa told me. And, since I can do an
hour's worth in twenty minutes, I've got plenty of time."

That kind of arrogance was meant to be tested.
"All right, here." She got off the stool and proffered him
her place. She stood in the doorway in full view of her
Pa. No use giving him cause to call her on some pretext
or other. She wanted to see those big, clumsy hands get
anything from her cow. Bessy would never be milked
that expertly that fast again.

"You're stayin' to supper?" Her question was matter of fact. One always asked that of a stranger at meal time.

"Probly."

Alfred would say, "If that is an invitation, I accept." Alfred displayed both wit and sophistication. Dummies said probly. If she had a big brother, He'd probly be a twin to Will.

He carried the milk nonchalantly on two fingers. She trailed behind, yet she passed him at the step, took the pail from him and put the door between them. Enough was enough. Maybe he wouldn't stay.

He did; and a new history unfolded.

TOUCH OF SNOW

Winter in Vermont brought snow, North wind, and sleigh bells. Covered bridges always took Hetty by surprise. Will was never a romantic; but he was a good provider, and he was gentle. His word was law just like her Dad's. McKenna's and Carradines were worlds apart in many ways. In common, they all took a touch of snow seriously. What began innocently could menace with days of drifting and piling up and considerable inconvenience.

Hetty took the rig on a partly cloudy day without consulting Will. She and the children would drive down to Werkville, a distance of twelve miles. "Don't bother Daddy, he's busy" were words she would regret. Beginning the ascent of the return trip, Hetty became aware of cloud shadows and a stiffening of the breeze. Then snowflakes, almost invisible, played tricks with her visibility.

Not an expert driver, Hetty grew anxious and
forgot Will's words, "When in doubt, give Charlotte her
reins. She's surefooted and knows the way." She
tightened her grip on the reins. Charlotte obeyed her
command and, crossing a large rut, broke the left rear
wheel. They were marooned seven miles from home.
Heavy snow would blanket them and cold would kill
them if they were not discovered. Of course they were.
Jason Lombard came over the rise, saw their distress and
packed them all in his wagon with extra blankets he
always kept stowed. With Charlotte in tow, the seven
miles were covered easily.

There was nothing for it but to face Will and be
grateful he was who he was. He said nothing. Only his
hard look conveyed the message that it wouldn't happen
again.

A barn always had at least one spare wheel. Her
assistance would be requested and she would learn.

Years later she would reflect on this beginning of
her thirst for knowledge and experience. Her expertise
in driving grandchildren began as an adventure that
could have been a disaster born of innocence. Reading
the weather became a top priority. She ever after talked
weather with old-timers.

OLD HICKORY

Jeffery and Susan were fair weather students at the county one room school three miles from home. The hickory stick was on prominent display, drilled and hung on a hook at the end of the chalk board. Study or else! No cheating, no whispering, QUIET spelled in capitals, no mischief, no fighting. The two Carradines knew their names meant nothing. Susan was no problem. Jeffery was another matter. Mr. Hawthorne's word was law, and Will and Hetty backed him all the way, as did every parent in the district. There was not a rule Jeffery had not broken at least once. He was a double dipper when it came to fighting.

Jeffery and William Pence took to name calling that escalated into fistfights.

The two of them made snide remarks in whispers until they were tanned and separated. Restraint was too much to ask of them. They were wild as mustangs and wildly resisted being broken. And, although Will saddled Jeffery with extra chores, he was secretly proud of the "like father, like son" being played out before him.

THE RELUCTANT PATIENT

The nose cold was drippy. The strained eyes and heavy head made Will edgy for a week and went away. His colds never lingered. Ginger and lemon schnapps in small doses kept him going.

Hetty took to her sewing or sorted her clothes. Laundry kept them apart, some getting done more than once. The chickens and her garden took up more of her time. She kept one eye on him from a distance. She could barely tolerate his disposition, a mild form of the boy who was a precursor to Jeffery.

After nine days his condition seemed to worsen. The argument over his seeing a doctor ended with her threat to move into the barn. He backed away from doing his own housework and cooking. But he was adamant about letting it run its course. The cold would go away as it always did. Blinders prevented him from seeing himself as others saw him.

He awoke weakened and with a chill. He could only repeat Hetty's name, a substitute for Mama. He was sweating. She felt his head. He was burning up.

Deliriously he kept repeating, "No doctor, no doctor."

The children would have to be kept home from school. Jeffery would have to ride Charlotte to summon Dr. Berg. Hetty could only fret and worry. She could only imagine the worst. She would have to take charge and make up for Will's distress.

Dr. Berg could only recommend complete rest and a palliative to make Will comfortable. Will had a strain of flue he picked up while in contact with a carrier. It was going around.

After two days the fever broke and the reluctant patient got up, put on his clothes and headed for the door. His knees buckled. He fell flat and called Hetty's name. She would spend two weeks trying to keep him down.

BLUE SCARF WEDDING

In the spring of 1887 Hetty turned seventeen. Will's stop over took on permanence, with a purpose, it would seem, of courting the farmer's daughter. She, on the other hand, would take a heap of persuading to compromise her independence and love this affable clod.

Will exhibited the patience it took to break a spirited filly and, only after months that lasted through the winter, did a thaw begin. Hetty began to see a dedicated suitor, though he had no visible means beyond board and keep and a few dollars a month that Papa would pay him.

Mama gave the appearance of being on his side. She was a great believer in things working out. A day in May Momma brought out something Hetty had never seen before. She fixed her eyes on what Momma described as the long, blue scarf. Momma wove a tale of something worn in the long ago of 1775. Betsy Worth got married on the fifth of June of 1775 amid the turmoil of Colonial unrest and British intrusion. Sergeant Clevon James was the nervous groom. Betsy was determined to declare her own independence from tradition by wearing the long, blue scarf she had acquired on a holiday to Boston. It was silk and accented her bosom beautifully.

"Hetty, when you marry, wear the heirloom. It has been traditional for family brides since that day in 1775."

A moonlight stroll finally put Will in the driver's seat. He had already asked her Pa for her hand. Papa was amiable and that roadblock had been overcome. When they paused, Will put his hand lightly on her shoulder and asked the question, quietly and seriously.

Hetty felt warm and uncomfortable. She would have to think it over.

"Take all the time you need."

No other words were spoken. Yet, in a space of two weeks and several bedroom chats with Momma, she made up her mind.

She took Will's hand and walked him to the veranda. She said, "I will if I can wear the blue scarf. She told Momma's story. Though he asked to see it, he could not. It would be bad luck.

"Wear what you will."

Bans were read.

On the fifth of June, 1888, Hetty stood before Will, Pa and Momma, and the Claybournes as witnesses. Momma had practiced "Pomp and Circumstance diligently and this was her moment. The minister stepped in from the ante room (kitchen). To his query she replied, "Oh, Will, I will."

The scarf would be folded and returned to its felt container and to Hetty's cedar chest. It came to mind of a Sunday when she looked at Susan and thought of Momma's surprise.

INHERITANCE AND BRAVE GOODBYES

Hetty was taken aback. Vermont! It might as well have been China. Will had dropped a bombshell. His uncle, Theodore, had passed and left him his spread, including thoroughbred horses. His means were secure and they would be moving there. To Vermont—a permanent honeymoon. The many discussions with Momma were warranted. Momma's own story helped Hetty to decide.

McKenna had taken homestead land in Dakota Territory in what would become Minor County. His need for a woman would reach by word of mouth to the Pacific Coast of Canada. Momma, who was orphaned at the age of twelve, became a ward of her Aunt Beth and Uncle Stanley. They worked her like Cinderella for her keep. Momma ran away from their cold, dispassionate discipline. She was sixteen. An elderly couple took her in as a helper and a traveling companion. They explained they were going home to Illinois to die. They gave themselves only a few years to live.

At an Idaho stop, she heard talk of the Dakota man. Was it the same man her aunt and uncle spoke of in her presence? She conjured up a picture of the man as one who was all she could hope for. Could they take her that far?

She addressed her message to the Dakota man in Minor County. He would meet the train in Fargo and "look her over".

"Fine for breeding," he said. Can you cook?"

"Better'in you've had since you left your Mamma."

"Guess we'll go over to the courthouse and get hitched if yer a mind to."

"You have to court me for a day or I'll go on."

"That's a price I can afford to pay if it'll get me a good woman. I'll take you to breakfast and we'll start from there."

She prayed until she fell asleep.

"I believe you were conceived the next evening, Hetty. You came to us nine months and two days later."

The master bedroom became a bridal suite. Hetty's parents retired to the straw mats in the barn and barred the door against intrusion. This was a good time for them to be alone together. They were good at it and the give and take had equal parts of love and determination to come to the exhausting end satisfied.

"Goodbye, goodbye, goodbye." Hetty and Mamma hugged and cried and clung to each other. Papa put a clumsy hand on her shoulder and spoke. "Have a good life. Write when you can. Maybe you can come and visit one of these years. Bring grand kids. We'd love to see 'em.

A happy journey mixed with remorse had begun.

TIMELESS AND SIMPLE

Days were made for timeless repetition that garnered expertise for passing on to new generations. Hetty bore well days that fit together like interesting puzzle pieces, well worn and easily recognized. Keeping busy subdued the urge to daydream. Now contentment spread over her like a mantle of faith; and daily prayer became as natural as breathing. She arose with God's mercy and love in her mind and a need to reach out with it to others. Those who knew her mind called on her, hoping a blessing would rub off on them.

Sara Payday, one day in June, announced her arrival with, "Hallooo! Anybody home? She could hear Hetty singing at her sewing even before she reached the stoop. She was one to carry tails up and down the valley and to chat an afternoon away, offering help in any way possible. Today, Sara told of the Beerless family's plight. They were forced out of their home and living with disagreeable relatives. Sara felt compelled to be their emissary, spreading the word.

Hetty made a note in her prayer list. Simply put, she would pray for them. Simply put, she would visit the household that held the victims of layoffs at the mill. Simply put, Hetty would weave it seamlessly into her timeless round of those things she kept in her heart and in her diary of her timeless routine.

She wanted always to take everyone under her wing who felt the sting of deprivation. But, she would heed the quiet "No" of Will, whose mantra was, "Take care of family first, near and far." He had said, "Take a pie and a blessing when you visit, but no more." As years passed, she felt completely comfortable under the Carradine brand.

STIFF AND SOBER PORTRAITS

The year held a January that continually produced heavy, drifting snow that isolated the individual homes from each other. Food was rationed. Feed was rationed. Livestock was kept indoors, especially during sub zero days and nights. It was a time of stinging winds and prayers they would ease.

The weather eased in time to usher in a February mini-spring with sunny days and gradual melting.

Hetty began to look forward with confidence to Easter Sunday. It just couldn't snow in an isolating way. She had her heart set on Church in town and, afterward, portraits. It was customary now for people to have their pictures taken by James Easton, a professional. Hetty had made her appointment a year ago. Easter Sunday had to be booked that far in advance.

Oh! Beautiful blue skies! Sunshine! A mother's prayer answered.

There was much to do about everything. Too excited, too hurried, the children snarked at each other after getting in each other's way. They had to do chores. They had to have breakfast. They had to don their new clothes. They had to pile out the door to the rig wearing dust covers. They were on their way to a line of rigs heading to town. The Carradine's had a fringed cover. Some were only buckboards pulled by a team. Their place in line was their place in line. There was no passing. The socializing could wait for the gathering at the church.

"Don't ruin your new clothes!" curbed the beginnings of games of tag. Prim and proper would be hard to maintain, though it must at all cost. It was a blessing that the two hour service was shortened.

No eating until after the pictures were taken. Sit quietly and read your book. Prisoners of portraiture passed the time catching up, visiting, penciling in their lives in the book of conversation that would be revisited in talk at home, all the while stiff and uncomfortable. Peevish children had to be corrected mid sentence. All of that energy with no place for it to go. "Wait until you get home!"

The photographs of the Carradines looked stiff and sober, Jeffery in front of Will and Susan in front of Hetty.

A TOUCH OF GINGER

It's not that rabbit was not plentiful. It made perhaps the best meat for stew. Susan had a good eye and could bring one down. Jeffery's aim was even better. Anyone related to Will Carradine learned to shoot accurately; though he was the one to bring home the buck or doe.

A small tome of twenty pages sold at Harrison's Mercantile for five cents—"Poet's Cookbook" b y A. J. Noth. It lay in a bin with other used books published in England in the 1850"s. Hetty picked it out, determined to try a few recipes.

At home of a Thursday, she gathered her ingredients for:

NO MEAT HATH THE STEW

Barley and beans and luck for a glue
Makes reliable vegetarian stew.
Apples can enhance the flavor, too.
No meat hath reliable vegetarian stew.
Go easy on the old peach brandy;
Save some for the vegetarian stew.
You are not making hard rock candy.

Some beans
Easy on the barley
Carrots
Onions
Potatoes
One parsnip

Add apples, peeled, cored and thickly sliced and ¼ cup of
peach brandy. Cover with water and simmer four hours.

A note said it went well with ginger snaps. Hetty
had made them that morning with flour, salt, sugar,
molasses and a touch of ginger.
The Carradines ate cookies and a taste of the stew.
Two butchering hogs had their fill.

THE REVEREND VISITS, CHURCH IS TRIED

The new Carradines had barely settled down on the property. Hetty's second thoughts had not yet been extinguished when the Reverend Peter Chancer paid a visit. It was his purpose to see the new bride and encourage regular attendance at the Church of the Redeemer, weather permitting.

Will stood in dust covered boots and work clothes. Hetty aproned and holding a duster welcomed the stranger. He looked a bit like the Alfred in her dreams in the hazy meadow. He was polite, well spoken, and had a certain charm in his demeanor. Hetty put down the duster and offered tea. Will could only wait impatiently but passively to get back to work. He would be at it, now, past supper time. His meal would be kept warm. It was the first time and the last time he would indulge an unannounced visitor. They could join him wherever his work took him. He and other men knew what was expected of them. They were present when the wife entertained anyone male.

The reverend was assured they would go of a Sunday, and with goodbyes, and talk, and goodbyes and talk he finally climbed into his rig and put Horse into a trot. He departed and made a right turn toward the Harringtons.

"I'll wait. We'll eat late," Hetty said. She was still of a mind the two of them would sit down together. Together they would be Carradines. She needed that identity. To him it was a matter of indifference.

They pulled up to the church, Charlotte a bit frisky but kept in check. Pleasantries were exchanged. The bell rang; and men extinguished cigars. Everyone filed into the sanctuary. Will knew the place from his youth and led the way to the pew with a Harrington nameplate. Ahems cleared throats. Otherwise extreme quiet prevailed, the kind that could be felt. Silence sat heavily

like fog and had a weighty density that made Hetty
hopeful the service would soon begin.

Reverend Chancer stepped to the lectern as
Joshua Biggs played the organ introit. Everyone stood
and bowed their heads. The opening prayer was lengthy
and full of thees, thou arts, and wilts and thankfulnesses
and a list of those who needed special care. The amens
again created the silence. Announcements and hymns
followed. A collection for missions was mostly coin; a
collection for the church was mostly coin. Big
contributors made monthly or yearly contributions. The
saloon keeper, Michael Mc Fee, was most generous, as
was the widow, Eleanor Carter. She paid Chancer's
salary and had his attentive ear.

The sonorous and serious sermon would be an
hour by the clock. It intoned, was full of clichés, and
repeated threats of condemnation by a jealous god.
Cotton Mather seemed to have mattered to the Reverend
Chancer, whose theology had been stamped with "Repent
or die!" man's low estate, worm-like in the scheme of
things.

Will said Chancer could take that sermon and
shove it. Then he was silent. They would not return for
three years, when the new reverend would be tried.
Eleanor Carter died, Chancer was sent packing to
another "calling" and the church took on a newness of
life. Man had value and became a co-creator. Will liked
that.

THE LEGEND OF SNAKE HOLLOW

(Will's camping tale told many times)

Jeffery and Will spent the summer weekend attending the father-son campout. Men and boys took to the woods to hunt, fish at Lake Wishnot, have ritual pissing contests, so Hetty thought, and indulge in other man activities.

Jeffery came in second in the junior wrestling contest. He lost out to Ken Akroyd who was two years older and twelve pounds heavier. It would be Ken's last time. Everyone gave way to age. Jeffery stood a good chance in a year to become King of the Hill.

Around the campfire Will brought up the Legend of Snake Hollow. He had the first timers, and it was his job to initiate them. He asked if any had heard the story. None had. All of the initiates were sworn to secrecy. It was an oath everyone kept to ward off dire consequences.

Will began: "There is, over the ridge there, a swamp dark and dangerous called Snake Hollow., a stinking swamp full of dead things killed by the slithering monster living in its lair. You new ones are going to have to sneak up on the monster and bring back proof you've seen it. You'll have to wait till it's asleep tonight, grab a whisker and run like the dickens. Don't get lost. Three boys over the years have never been seen again. Everybody who is chicken gets tied to a tree naked and embarrassed no end. It's time to prove your manhood."

Half believing, scared, trembling, the four boys moved reluctantly toward the ridge. They could see steam rising or a fog gathering near the ground. Over the ridge and down into the hollow they crept. They heard hissing and gurgling. As they crept closer, they made out the shape, long, with a giant head.

The shape at last lay still, its breathing rhythmic in sleep. Mark Cupple drew the short straw and, shaking and trebling, crawled toward the monster. He got near the sleeping beast, reached out and, ready to run, he made a plucking motion at a long hair. Will in disguise reached up and grabbed the boy and shouted, "Gotcha." The long straws ran for all they were worth, yelling gibberish as they neared the camp. Will followed carrying Mark on his shoulders.

They all snacked on treats, even the quivering, before the fire was extinguished and sleep overtook all, including the monster.

Snake Hollow would be safe for another year.

CHARLOTTE DIES

Susan was three and loved her horsey. She loved her pseudo gift presented while on a picnic outing. She sat next to Mama who said, "Look at the horsey, Susan's horsey." Charlotte was twenty-two, still able to take the carriage for a spin to the stream and back, some two miles. Jeffery went because he got to fish for crappies.

In the fall the horsey labored with plodding steps. Charlotte was pastured and a deal was struck with the rendering plant. Will was not sentimental about any of the animals. They pulled their weight or they were destroyed. Hetty was determined in this case to make an exception. She argued that Susan could not see her horsey suddenly gone.

"And who made Charlotte her horsey?" was Will's response.

"Of course, I did. I take the blame for that. But it's not fair to her now. I'm sure Charlotte won't last much longer."

In a week Charlotte was found on her side unresponsive. Now Susan could be told that Charlotte simply went away. It was God's will.

OUT OF THE PAST

The tree was widening considerably. Hetty
Carradine sat in her favorite wicker chair with cushions.
A half moon accent table stood next to the chair, its
drawer half open. Hetty was seventy. She sat
comfortably waiting for a blessed event to take place, the
Christening of her great granddaughter, Elizabeth Alice
Martin.

It had been two years and three weeks since Will's
funeral. She went on. Jeffery, single at fifty-five, ran the
stables. Susan and John Martin begat Jonathon, who,
with Clara, begat Elizabeth.

History came in snapshots over many years; and a
trove was stored in the crescent drawer. Hetty took
several from a packet and fingered them slowly away,
each revealing another. The wall clock's pendulum
ticked away the time. It was Sunday. Hetty's mind
enveloped each scene she held before her eyes.

One was the McKenna's last day at the homestead.
The property had been sold to a farming combine led by
Jesse Payne. Mother and dad moved to Vermillion in
Retirement. The Carradines were there that day; the
only time the McKenna's saw the nearly grown Jeffery
and Susan. The talk never ceased and catching up put
their lives in perspective. The farmhouse was well kept
and as sturdy as ever. A cow could be seen being herded
toward a trailer. Not much remained. The auction had
been good. Will bought a relic, the old plow, to ship back
as a remembrance. Nothing had gone to ruin.

Hetty packed what was personal for the trip back
to Vermont. The picture she fingered put in her mind the
Easter Sunday photograph. It had never left its mantle
place, and the cracked lower right corner of the glass told
of its travel to South Dakota. Now it had a new mantle
place, its glass not replaced.

Jeffery studied and studied and won a spelling bee. Twenty years later he stood stiffly posed, holding the certificate, while Hetty took his picture.

Susan stood with her deviled eggs at an Easter breakfast.

Will, in a black suit and tie, wearing a western style hat, held the bridle of a black stallion name Champ, a name Jeffery gave the horse. It had never entered a race much less won.

Hetty seated in the rig with a tight grip on slack reins squinted a little into the sun.   Picture after picture uncovered the past and renewed Hetty's spirit. Her life had been full, though it was not quite complete.

"Grandma, it's almost time. We'll have new pictures for the collection in just a short while." Hetty placed her pictures on the table where they would be when she returned. History could be interrupted but not easily turned off.

Flashbulbs introduced Elizabeth to the recorded history of the Carradines.

OLD HETTY SPEAKS

Hetty was back at her place by the crescent table. This time she had been given Elizabeth to hold. The two of them had contentment written all over them. Two photographs lay on the table, first the infant Susan on Hetty's lap, then Jonathon. Liz' picture would join them. Hetty had rehearsed her speech for this moment.

"Little Lizzy, times are different now. You will be free to make your own choices. You won't have to marry your boss. You won't have to take a back seat in the affairs of men. I see you a Congresswoman, even the President. Don't be afraid to speak your mind. Wear pants if it suits you. You could run a business, even this one. Learn to ride. Learn to shoot. Be an Annie Oakley. Maybe you should leave here and take on the world. But, never forget who you are. Though your name is Elizabeth Alice Martin, you will always be a Carradine. The Carradine brand is something you can steer by.

HETTY'S LITTLE HELPER

Women's work, and Susan was caught in the middle. She did not take to the harness gladly, but resisted with a glum look that could be interpreted as a feeling of being cheated. Hetty thanked heaven for a little girl who would eventually be a little helper.

Susan at nine began to take on features resembling her mother and was prettier with a smaller nose and dark tresses. It was then that she began to dawdle in front of a mirror, forgetting the time and the chore to be done.

Hetty remembered her father's words, though they were not enough. She could not whistle; but she could make a whoo-whoo sound. She called herself the engine and Susan the little caboose that could. Susan would follow Hetty about the house from one chore to another. Hetty would fetch Susan and chug her to her next chore. After a month, though less frequently, the game continued on an as necessary basis. Susan could smile more readily as she learned the benefits of hypocrisy. And Hetty did not reveal that she knew.

CHARLOTTE ON LOAN

Werkville's Founder's Day found the mayor, James beadle, short of a ride in the Founder's Day Parade. Viewers watched three or four floats on trailers, the school kids marching behind the town's volunteer band, the Equestrian Brigade in colorful outfits, uniformed veterans and the mayor and his wife.

Bridie, the mayor's horse came up lame the day before the parade. Members of the Equestrian Brigade knew where to go. Charlotte came to mind as an unequaled substitute. John Bingham rode up to the Carradine place to ask for Charlotte on loan.

There was some haggling over price. Will wanted twenty dollars and a letter as a surety bond against harm to the horse that guaranteed payment up to the horse' value, one hundred and thirty dollars. He accepted a guarantee of eighty-two dollars plus rental fee of twenty-five dollars.

Charlotte wore the "horse's hat" with ear cutouts. She took to the clopping plod easily and seemed to enjoy the crowd noise and the attention. It was then that Hetty thought of Charlotte as a horsey.

Word got to Hawks, ten miles to the north. Checkers, the horse that pulled the carriage of the festival queen, was sold. His replacement was not ready in time for the parade. Again a deal was struck and Charlotte, this time, strutted with her head high, evoking applause. For two years she put her best foot forward in both towns. Then age suddenly caught up with her the year Susan was born. After three years, Susan's horsey "went to pull a chariot in the sky."

DAD'S LITTLE SECRET

Susan, at six, wanted a piglet for her birthday. At six or seven all the little girls wanted them for pets. Of course, a great deal was made of nixing the idea. Even Hetty, who thought it romantic to have a little porker running around the place, even eating off a plate on the floor, talked of the idea being nonsense.

Susan, jealous of Mila and Betty who already had them, sulked for days. It was certain she would be denied. She knew better than to rely on her Dad.

Will was practical, not sentimental. Though he never committed to anything frivolous, Hetty saw something in his eyes that was disturbing. When confronted, Will confessed to seeing a profit in selling the no longer cute pig when Susan's "phase" had run its course. So, on her birthday Susan's dad was gone. She was told he had to go to the Herman's to help them with a spirited horse. Long after the hogs were butchered peach brandy remained. The Herman's daughter, Jess, had outgrown her piggy, Hermione. The peach brandy was a part of the payment and therein lay the profit. And Will was invited to help down a pint, which he kept as his little secret, shared only with Hetty.

THREE DAYS OF FRIED CHICKEN

It was outside the parameters of hospitality to refuse invitations to dinner, especially if you were new neighbors. Will made it clear there could be no excuses; though Hetty was anxious to meet everyone and become a part of the social mix. Their first month in their new home had a dozen invitations, offers they could not refuse. Yet there was so much to do! Tired would have to be put off. Hetty could feel "bone tired" coming on. What would reciprocation be like?

Yet, women visited her to get a peek at her and satisfy their curiosity; and they made themselves useful, helping getting things done. Conversations went along in waltz-time on the heels of chores. Hetty learned their easy way for housekeeping, leaving time for tea and relaxation that conversation spilled into. Housewives came and issued invitations to dinner. Myra Madison came on a Thursday, the day after their arrival. The following Thursday Hetty and Will were off to the Madison's, riding in dress-up and hats Hetty demanded for social calls. Will had said no need to bother. Hetty insisted she show off her best. Ed and Myra were as casual as they come. Weather and planting and foals and up-state trotters were topics of discussion. Will was content and at home in his element. Hetty was content to listen. Then she was asked about her Dakota life and reminiscences came again to mind, as they would over the years. She thought about Mama's fried chicken. Then Myra came to the table with a large platter of her own fried chicken, done for this special occasion.

Friday they were due at the Comstock's for dinner. They would be casually dressed this time. They arrived. Will and Buck had their whiskey before all were seated around the table for a fried chicken surprise. Hetty could only compliment a different recipe.

Saturday the newcomers joined a gathering outside of the town park for picnic and games. Lulu Belle supplied the main dish, finger licking good fried chicken. Hetty had a wing. Will ate heartily to belt-tightening satisfaction. He simply had a weakness for fried chicken and everyone knew it.

THE NEW REVEREND'S HOBBY

The new reverend, Charles Knudsen, a liberated Lutheran, made it known, while introducing his first sermon, that he was not only a fisher of men but a fisher of fish. He created adornments for hooks. He had even created a few rods, having observed his father creating them. This was good news for men and boys, and, for two women, one of whom was Hetty. Will not only taught hunting but fishing as well. Hetty could help him catch a meal. The other female was Gretchen Army, a heathen who attended church to honor her mother and father. She wore men's clothes and palled with and held hands with several young ladies, secretly. She had won more than one fishing contest. Hetty, then, had an excuse to get to know her. Hetty would not be a hand holder but would like to be a friend to everyone.

People accepted that Will made Hetty a Carradine in as many ways as possible. Fishing was as Carradine as being able to hunt or handle horses. The last she demurred to Will and shied away until the incident with 'Charlotte.

On the first outing the Reverend patronized her as one who seemed out of place, though she had her own rod and ties. After she landed three more than he, he had a new respect for one he could only wish could be Mrs. Knudsen. Secret loves were not new to him. They only served to focus him on his two high callings, the business of the Lord and mastering the art of fishing.

PICKLED IS PICKLED

Everything has its scripture, and canning time was no exception. Rhubarb was packed in canning jars with lots of sugar. Berries made thick preserves. Dill seed and brine produced some dill pickles that Will devoured, not always with consideration for his stomach. He would pop one in his mouth after a jar was opened, bite off a large chunk and squint his eyes before scrunching them shut, savoring what, to Hetty, should have choked him. Two pickles and he needed a teaspoon of baking soda diluted in water to settle his stomach "queezies". The headache snuck up on him and he had to lie down for an hour. And who smoothed his furrowed brow? Nurse Hetty, she of the home-remedy knowhow passed down from her mother. Jonny and Ely were her practice patients.

Imbibing rum was less seasonal. Men had a tendency to sit around after dinner and mix palaver with homemade formulas. On a few occasions Will was left lightheaded and unsteady, as was his companion in conversation. Myra Madison had a name for it. "Pickled is pickled," she would say.

BROWNIES AT THE PICNIC

Soon after the turn of the century an explosion of invention occurred that gave prominence to "must-haves" for households in the county. Carradines were no exception. They were among the first families to have a horseless carriage which Will got a bang out of every time he cranked it. Kitty Hawk made front page news. And, Brownies were everywhere. Jeffery, the stay-at-home had one of his own.

On a June Sunday for Col. George Strathmore, in the park, one found the use of Brownie cameras wherever one looked. The Civil War veteran was honored every year on a Sunday near the anniversary of the battle in which he exhibited extraordinary gallantry and heroism. He had singlehandedly held off a charge by Rebs while his unit retreated. It cost him his life. His bronze statue depicting him astride his steed was the target of many photos that day.

The Brownie "waltz" carried ladies with their parasols and their gentlemen on promenades about the park, meeting, photographing each other, putting "lazy" to work prior to placing blankets and sitting upon them to consume lunches.

People alternately stood to take pictures of their families or groups. Discussion took place about what to shoot, how to get the best pictures, what instruction had been gleaned from Eastman and other professional photographers. The convenient Brownie seemed to sell itself. Will, however, patiently put up with the nonsense, though he did admire the way he looked when Jeffery caught him candidly and unaware until the camera clicked his image. He was simply lounging under an oak and casually paring his nails with a pocket knife.

The old Hetty held that picture carefully for a long time before returning it to her "memory box".

JONNY'S MOVE TO A JOB IN TOWN

Jonny was courting the barber's daughter in Centerville according to letters from Mama. He had moved from the homestead to town. During the Carradine visit, the pair showed up to show off and to aid with the sale.

Jonny McKenna was bright and high spirited. He lifted Hetty off the ground with a hug, tightly wound and enthusiastic, laughing a greeting that made her flushed and a little embarrassed. He had to recount the details of his move; and at dinner he boisterously elaborated.

Centerville was now a wagons west stop and had two general stores and three saloons. It even had an apothecary. Jonny worked behind the counter. He learned the names of various nostrums and cure-alls and their uses. He met Jenny Jewison, the daughter of Mason Jewison, a barber, when she came into the store to buy something for her sore throat. The doctor had prescribed horehound, a camphor rub-on and a mustard plaster. After her cure, she kept coming in with excuses for talking to him about what was good for what. "Who was good for whom" would have been a better question.

Jonny was the one who swept the place and locked up. Often he would make his way to the Jewison home rather than to his room at Mrs. Hempton's boarding house. He and Jenny would sit together, not saying much sometimes. It took a while for him to hold her hand and get a bit tingly and uncomfortable. Familiarity bred a kiss until a kiss was not just a kiss, as time went by.

IRA'S BIRTHDAY PANCAKES

Ira, Mama's baby, in the days leading up to his being nine years old, was often lost in thought and one time got himself lost and put everyone in a panic. Out of reach of hearing, he was doing what his father told him to do, "taking a hike".

Lost in thought, Ira got off the beaten path and wandered until he became disoriented. Unfortunately he did not stay put but wandered in trial and error that only kept him out of hearing range. Then he sat discouraged and tearful and hungry.

Twelve hours went by. He had slept. Then reality set in. He was really alone. This time his crying was heard. Hetty found him, three miles from home, sitting next to a tree with his back to the wind. She held him tight for a long time before she led him along the stream bed and home.

Hetty remembered telling him it was his birthday. While he had slept, he turned nine. "What kind of cake shall we make?" she asked; her own joyful tears made her voice tremble.

Pancakes!" he shouted. I want pancakes." All had a hearty breakfast of pancakes.

ELIZABETH ONE

Hetty walked with a cane slowly and carefully to the dinner table. She was tired from the Christening, the pictures and visiting. There had not really been time to rest. After a moment of silence, after the grace, she broke in with talk of her great aunt. Everyone by now knew the story. Yet it was important to her that everyone be reminded.

"My great aunt was the first Elizabeth in our family. My grandmother's sister was given that name."

There was more, but she did not speak further and sat silently with her memory as the conversation went toward her great granddaughter, the need for an early start for family who had to get home.

Hetty had only met her great aunt once, when Elizabeth and her husband, Albert, migrated from Nova Scotia to the Kansas prairie. Hetty must have been seven at the time. "Aunt" Elizabeth spoke of Carradines who were neighbors up north. Hetty had forgotten that immediately and not remembered even when she met Will as a hired hand. It came to her one wash day perhaps twelve years later.

Will said he knew of no Carradines beyond their Vermont home; and Hetty was satisfied with that. It only came back repeatedly as she aged. Repeats were an accepted part of who she was now. In her mind Elizabeth 2 looked like Elizabeth I, with fine features and delicate hands. Perhaps she would find a "Carradine" of her own.

STOP ME IF YOU'VE HEARD THIS ONE

Busy swept into Hetty's life; and kept her imagination alive. Her life with Will was, for the most part, all she could have hoped for, and children kept her an hour short every day, time not regained until Sunday afternoon and a two hour nap, Sunday dinners notwithstanding.

As they aged, children's needs were confined to home time. Busy was no longer exhausting. School time lessened the burden of perpetual motion and, unbidden, a vision of Alfred would enter her mind once or twice as she baked bread or tended flowers or had busy hands at some task. Her hands could work with little prompting or attention to detail.

He stood as if suspended in air, an apparition, staring at the sixteen year old and told her of his life; but he also told things designed to tickle her sense of humor. Not an imaginary lover, he was companionable and befriended her at times when she wished Will were there.

Alfred was trim, well tailored and English through and through. His blond mustache curled slightly upward. He was a Devonshire lad, well bred, and Oxford educated. Of course he was dashing. Hadn't Hetty dreamed him up years ago?

During his first visitation, Alfred chuckled and said, "Stop me if you have heard this one. There once was a maid so plain her mirror was turned to the wall. She had to walk backward to keep from frightening children. Her corset was so tight it burst and she literally fell out of it, to the dismay of her companion who very much wanted to marry her....for her money! Her saving grace was one million pounds and sixpence. The sixpence she saved since she was five in her little piggy....."

"Oh, Alfred, stop!"

" Where'd Alfred come from?" Will stood in the kitchen doorway. "What'd he have to say?"

Hetty had told him early in their marriage of her witty but twitty (Will's word) Alfred.

"Well, it was about a plain looking woman. I guess I've told it before." Please stop me if you've heard this one.

DANCING UNDER THE STARS

Early teens caused romance to bloom in Hetty's mind. She earned money for "Dance Steps" via post from Kansas City. She practiced faithfully, partnered with Alfred who was surprisingly light as air. The waltz was easy; and she stepped and twirled, charmed by her partner's wit and grace.

Then along came the size twelve shoes, the rough hands, large and daunting. She put away her dancing shoes with the shiny buttons and did up her hair and took on the age of a woman. At least in appearance. A few times Alfred would not come when she whispered his name.

She was anxious to try out the cotillion in Centerville and dazzle the public with her ability. That never happened. But, as she and Will made the rounds and were passed from dinner to dinner, she had the chance to waltz around a spacious living room to the admiration of the Selby's. John Selby was quite a dancer and always the gentleman. Will never asked her to dance. She did not know if he could. Yet, he suddenly cut in and his thumb gently caressed her fingers as her hand lay along his palm. This awakening thundered in her ears. Suddenly it was imperative they dance together. In her mind she had discovered a Will of her dreams. And she began to love him deeply. Yet it was months before she could coax him to take her to the Pavilion newly built in the valley.

On a cool clear evening in June she nagged him into wearing his white tails and rakish hat for dancing under the stars.

PARLOR TRICKS

Harry Lauder was a frequent guest on "The Parlor Hour", a radio program dedicated to parlor songs. Not so engaged with busy, Hetty took tea and played solitaire while the announcers brought in the funny, the witty urbane, the serious that could nudge a tear. She loved the exaggerated brogue with the charming trill. Will still puttered and bought and sold horses. Jeffery took care of chores and generally managed the place.

The war was over. Peace in the valley was now, not someday. Hetty could catch a few winks and wake to the closing song. More often than not the singer was Harry.

Like the Brownie camera, the household radio took the country by storm as early broadcasts took on the mystery of magic.

The time that the young visitor interrupted the Parlor Hour brought a smile to Hetty's face. She remembered the ten year old had straw colored hair and freckles. He was just clean and shiny as a new penny. They were neighbors of a sort; and his father came to dicker with Will over the sale of a chestnut stallion. Jonny Timbruck asked Hetty if she would like to see his magic trick. She said of course she would and twinkled with her eyes the way ladies have always charmed youngsters.

In flipping the coin between his fingers, Jonny accidently lost the coin, and it bounced on the carpet. "Wait, do-overs, watch."He was finally able to capture the coin in his palm, close his fist and make the coin disappear. During his card trick he lost the shuffle, and cards scattered. Three times he tried before succeeding and having her pick a card and guessing it wrong, though she said it was her card. Pleased, he left her when his father called.

She did catch the last song, even if Parlor Hour had become parlor tricks from a budding practitioner of legerdemain.

CHECKERS BEFORE DAWN

When Checkers became the game board rage, Jonny and Ira were old enough to be competitive and were trying to beat each other, whether it was bending willows the hardest, throwing stones the furthest, wrestling until "uncle" was voiced, or capturing men from the Checker Board.

The boys slept on cots in the kitchen and pulled blankets over themselves after the fire in the stove died and the ashes went cold. Usually they slept soundly and had to be pried from their cots to begin chores in time to walk to the one room school.

Hetty could see them again the day they woke just before dawn. The clacking noise had awakened her; and she crept from bed to investigate. Mama and Poppa came behind her. There were the boys, huddled under their blankets, clacking furiously as they jumped their opponent's "men". They had really intended to be quiet. As in everything else, they threw caution to the wind and took no quarter; and "king me!" was shouted before they realized they had an audience.

The rosy glow of the morning sun trumped their game, and scolding just seemed wrong at the time. Papa did pry them from the floor, told them to put the game away, and sent them off to begin their chores.

Hetty told the story often. Vermonters were great story tellers and great listeners. It was no surprise, then, that Jeffery and Susan one morning, pre-dawn, were engaged in the clacking racket that brought Hetty and Will to the door of Jeffery's room. Blankets were wrapped around them. Susan's "king me" was shrill and belligerent. Hetty could only laugh, and Will could only be silent. Later he would ask Hetty if she would like to get even.

Early the next morning the two of them huddled with blankets around themselves and clacked.

HETTY'S BIG HANG-UP

Hetty's parents were not religious, but they were God fearing, especially where their children were concerned. Hetty, Jonny and Ira were taught not to take the Lord's name in vain. God fearing and Papa fearing were one and the same. They knew in no uncertain terms where Papa stood on the subject of swearing. In her childhood Mamma had heard it all and was repulsed by it.

When provoked to an exclamation to condemn something, Hetty came out with the words, "peanut butter!" It seemed to suffice and incurred no wrath. Momma even adopted it.

When the telephone came to Vermont, crank calls were made and received daily. The hand crank on the phone had to be spun initially. When Leticia Marks called Hetty on a Saturday morning, it was to invite herself to brunch, and she would bring her peanut butter sweet rolls, made with butter and topped with peanuts.

Hetty put the receiver on the hook and laughed uncontrollably. Then she cranked the phone and called Leticia to apologize and explain the big swear she had invented and to accept the invitation to play host.

ANOTHER CAN OF WORMS

It was Jeffery's introduction to alcohol that bothered Hetty, even though it was not entirely Will's fault. The two guys had gone fishing upstream. Jeffery, with his father, had a favorite fishing hole not far from a bend near some shade trees. Jeffery was fifteen and felt independent enough to go around the bend, out of sight of Will.

When Will found him after about thirty minutes, Jeffery was sitting on the ground inattentive to his fishing pole and slumped against a tree. Between his legs was an empty scotch bottle. Will shook him until he was coherent enough to respond to questioning. He had found the bottle by the tree two thirds empty and, out of curiosity, and out of Will's sight, thought he would taste it. Sip after sip emptied the bottle of its contents and Jeffery was inebriated.

Usually they were away an hour or two and brought small catches for a fish fry. Now it was worry time. Four hours, five hours, seven hours before they finally appeared. Jeffery had become ill. Will had waited until he had slept it off. Then Jeffery had sobered and become hungry. The lateness led to their fish fry over hot coals which they had to be sure were out. Then they engaged in throwing rocks at the bottle until Jeffery broke it. Then they had to clean up the glass and bury it. Then they had to catch more fish to make up for the ones eaten. Then they had to pack their gear and head for home. It was Jeffery who had to confess to Hetty the nature of their outing and his Imbibing of the spirits.

"Well, Peanut Butter! You worried me sick. I can live with an extended stay. But, getting drunk is another can of worms. Do it again and I'll have you making beds." Susan, a little pitcher in the kitchen, snickered loudly.

HUNTING FOR LILA

It was a cloudy, blustery day that Lila disappeared. Hetty must have been twelve or thirteen. A stray white dog visited the homestead and was cared for and stayed on. It was companionable and a snake catcher and a furry female that was given the name, Lila. Papa said when she misbehaved she would lie like a rug to get out of it.

Hetty's mind would drift now and she slept more. Age was taking its toll. A recurring dream put her back with the dog and the walks they had together. They played tug-of-war with a stick and engaged in running a short way, only to flop down and wrestle playfully. She loved Lila as much as anyone in the family.

Then Lila was gone. Hetty walked in all directions calling the dog to no avail. After three weeks, everyone gave up on ever seeing her again. Finally the dream had a happy ending. After searching for days, the same scene repeating itself several times, she found Lila. The dog was a little bloodied and scarred but healthy and playful as ever. Even as Hetty awakened, the vision of the dog remained until her mind cleared, and Lila would need to be sought again.

A DARK, RICH BLEND

Elizabeth was a 5' 2" and a mighty-mite who took on her corner of Africa in a whirlwind delight. Her mission as a member of "Volunteers of the Church of the Supreme Being" was to aid the poor and the sick at the church sponsored clinic in Nairobi. She just took on affairs of the heart and poured herself into her work. She negotiated speaking engagements, and her lectures inspired the wealthy to make substantial contributions to meet the needs of slum dwellers. Often she spent twelve hour days processing patients. She quickly learned the language and the dialect of those she served and was able to translate fluently to English speaking doctors.

Now 22, Elizabeth had not seen her mother in four years, though she and Grandma, Susan, corresponded with monthly letters. Flying home now made her sad. Her sense of relief and anticipation of seeing family was tempered by her Mother's call. Gram had passed away. A very frail Hetty had reached out an arm, said, "Oh, Will, I will" and had stopped breathing.

On the flight she sipped her coffee. Her mind processed the stories that had been told, in Liz' early years by Hetty and, later, by Susan. The vignettes of a life that told of early years in South Dakota, of marriage and Vermont and a horse named Charlotte, of one Hetty Carradine, some humorous, some painful, some borne with grace and dignity. Elizabeth compared that life to her coffee, a dark, rich blend.